Big Girls Do It
Pregnant

JASINDA WILDER

BIG GIRLS DO IT PREGNANT

ISBN: 978-0-9891044-1-8
Copyright © 2013 by Jasinda Wilder

To my five beautiful children, because you taught me the joy of being a mother.

Chapter 1: Anna

JEFF GROANED IN FRUSTRATION, scrubbing his face with one hand. "Again, Anna? We've barely gone a hundred miles."

I sighed. "I'm sorry, Jeff. It's not like I can help it, you know."

He glanced at the GPS unit attached to the windshield beneath the rearview mirror. "Can't you hold it a bit longer? The city isn't that far away."

I shook my head. "I've *been* holding it. I had to go an hour ago—I just didn't say anything. Now I *have* to go, and no, I can't make it all the way downtown."

Jeff blew air out between his lips. "Never gonna make it to New York at this rate," he muttered under his breath as he began merging across traffic toward the interstate exit. "Stop to pee every hour, need a snack every half hour. Jesus."

I laughed. "Quit complaining, Jeff. I wanted to fly, but no, you didn't think it was safe."

"The doctor said no flying during the last trimester. You're five months. I don't want to take any chances."

I slipped my hand under his. "And I get that. I appreciate your concern for me and our baby. But if you want to take a road trip with a pregnant woman, you have to know the risks. It's not like you haven't been living with me peeing and eating all the time for the last twenty weeks."

He huffed again as he pulled into a McDonalds parking lot. "I know, I know. I didn't even want to go to New York in the first place. And now it's taking double the amount of time it should because you've suddenly got the bladder of a fucking chipmunk."

I snorted. "And you're an expert on chipmunk bladders now? What if chipmunks can hold it forever?" I shoved open my door and heaved myself up and out. I wasn't a beached whale yet, but movement was getting more difficult every day. "And I know you didn't want to go, Jeff. But it's Jamie's baby shower. I can't miss it."

I closed the door on his grumbling about parties for babies who weren't even born yet, laughing at him still. Jamie was having her baby shower in

New York City a lot sooner than normal because Chase's tour was hitting Madison Square Garden, and he wouldn't be home again until she was about to pop.

I peed and got back in the Yukon, settling in for the last leg of our trip. Jeff grumbled a lot, but was always sweet and understanding. He'd dealt with my craziness for weeks now, and his complaints were always in good humor. If I asked him to get me a snack at two in the morning, he would. Fortunately, I hadn't had a lot of odd cravings so far. Mainly, I was hooked on Triscuits and cheese and sparkling lime water. Like, a box of crackers and a block of cheese a day, that kind of hooked. Jeff was buying the lime water by the case from Whole Foods. I also couldn't stand the smell or taste of chicken, tuna, or nail polish. I hadn't painted my nails since about the eleventh week, which was driving me nuts, as I'd been getting weekly or biweekly mani-pedis for years. I even tried pinching my nose and having Jeff paint my nails, but the smell lingered in the air and made me nauseous anyway. And I was already nauseous all the time, so that sucked. Once, when Jeff made himself a tuna sandwich, I nearly barfed and started yelling at him so bad he actually took the tuna and threw it out the back door so I'd stop shrieking at him. Of course I couldn't go outside until he'd cleaned that up, which sucked since I liked to sit on the porch and read.

The other truly awful part of being pregnant, so far, was that I had zero sex drive. Just none. No motivation whatsoever. It wasn't that I found Jeff suddenly unattractive or anything; I was just nauseous all the time, and if I wasn't nauseous, I was tired or cranky, or some other combination of ridiculous hormonal imbalances. Which, of course, translated into a cranky, testosterone-ridden Jeff. He refused to take care of things himself, for some odd reason. He couldn't or wouldn't explain his aversion to it, except that he believed, since he was married to me, that he wouldn't do that, even if it meant going weeks without sex. I kept telling him I wouldn't mind, since I just couldn't get in the mood for even a hand job, let alone a BJ.

I tried to go down on him once, actually. It was about fifteen weeks in, and I was feeling okay that day. Jeff had been especially sweet, bringing me tulips and chocolate when he got back from work. I wanted to reward him for being so nice, especially after he rubbed my feet for twenty minutes. So after we'd gotten in bed, I ran my fingers along his bare stomach, pushed off his boxers, and fondled him into erection.

His lips curved into a lazy smile as I glided my fingers around him, and then he sighed when I slid on my side down his body until my face was level with his shaft. I had him going, pumping him steadily until his hips began to move in time with my strokes. *So far, so good*, I thought. No nausea, no roiling in my stomach. Finally, as he was nearing climax, I took him in my mouth, shallowly at first, just the tip past my lips, sucking gently, cupping his balls and stroking his base still. He was groaning and sighing my name, and I felt good giving my man what he needed.

He tugged gently on my hair twice, crying out, "Oh, god, Anna, yes...don't stop, please...I'm coming now—god, thank you, thank you—" And then his voice trailed off into a wordless cry of release as he shot weeks'-worth of pent-up come into my throat.

When he came, he came *hard*. Like a firehose, straight down my esophagus. Usually that was fine. I don't think that's any girl's favorite thing ever, despite what I've heard some chicks claim. I mean, how could it be anyone's favorite thing? Even when you're ready for it, it's surprising. Jeff always tasted good to me, never bitter or too musky, and I really, truly didn't mind going down on him. I usually enjoyed the feeling of making him lose control, giving him such pleasure. I may not have found the actual experience erotic for myself, as in, I didn't get off on giving him head, but it was something I enjoyed doing for him.

I was suitably shocked, then, when I went from pleased with myself and loving Jeff's frantic gasping and groaning and almost pathetically desperate whispered thanks as he came in my mouth to sudden and violent nausea.

It was like being shot by a vomit-cannon. The thick, salty, musky seed hit my throat and the back of my tongue, and instantly I felt my gorge rising. I wasn't gagging as if he'd pushed himself too deep; it was an immediate sickness.

I literally leapt off him, his cock leaving my mouth with an audible *pop*, and scrambled off the bed, barely making it into the bathroom before I heaved violently into the toilet.

Jeff—god bless the amazing man—was right there beside me, holding my hair back. He was panting, naked, still half-erect, and confused, but he was still thinking of me.

Even as I puked again, I felt a rush of love for him.

"I'm sorry," I gasped, glancing up at him between heaves. "It wasn't you, baby, I promise, I just...oh, god—" and then I lost it once more, heaving until my now-empty stomach turned it into futile retching.

He held my hair with one hand, snatched a washcloth off the towel rack with the other, and wetted it down under the sink—which wouldn't mean much to most people, unless you knew that I tended to get sweaty after vomiting. Jeff had knelt beside me often enough at that point in the pregnancy to know this about me. He helped me sit back on my ass on the cold tile floor of the bathroom and wiped my face with the washcloth, brushing stray tendrils of my blonde hair out of the way. I was gasping for air, clutching my still-tumbling stomach, groaning and praying that the nausea would pass.

When I finally thought it was gone, I struggled to my feet, clutching to Jeff for dear life. He helped me back to bed, slipped on his underwear, and cradled me against his broad chest.

"I'm sorry, Anna. I should have known that would make you sick. I shouldn't have let—"

I cut him off. "I wanted to, Jeff. I really did. It just hit me really suddenly. I was fine all the way up until you came, and then I was just sick, like, instantly. I don't know if I can do that again, though."

He sighed. "No kidding."

I couldn't help a little laugh at the wistful tone in his voice. "I really am sorry, Jeff. I know I've not really been in the mood lately. Hopefully the morning sickness phase will pass at some point."

He smoothed my hair away, and when he spoke his voice was heavy with sleep. "It's fine, baby. I'll live."

"Yeah, but you'll be cranky-horny all the time until I give it to you again," I said, sleepy now myself.

I barely registered his lazy grunt in response as I fell asleep.

After that, I hadn't even tried. I'd joined him the shower once, a week before we left for New York, and got him off with my hand, but when he tried to return the favor, I found myself unable to find a release. Eventually he gave up, both of us frustrated.

Now, with my feet sticking out the open car window to rest on the side-view mirror, I realized I hadn't been nauseous yet that day, or the day before. I hadn't puked in almost a week, actually. I glanced at Jeff, who had his chin propped on one hand and the other wrist draped over the steering wheel. As I watched, he absently took his hand off the wheel, reached down, and adjusted himself inside his gym shorts.

Watching that, the brief movement of his hand tugging himself into a more comfortable position, or whatever it is guys do when they adjust their junk like that, I felt a twinge of something that could have been desire. It also may have been heartburn from having eaten McDonalds for the last five out of eight meals, but I was pretty sure it was desire.

I didn't say anything, I just tilted my seat farther back, rested my head on an angle so I could watch Jeff without being obvious about it. See, this whole no sex for the last three months thing had been shitty for me, too. I wanted to want him. I'd gotten used to having Jeff whenever I wanted him, daily, or nearly daily. Some days we'd both be busy or tired, but we'd never, since first getting together, gone more than a week without some kind of sexual liaison, whether it was actual intercourse, oral sex, or just groping hands and kissing. So this whole *I want to want you but can't* business was getting old for me, too. I watched him drive and tentatively imagined myself reaching over the console and touching him, perhaps just exploring the muscle and skin and dusting of hair on his belly at first. That went well. The picture fit, as it should. I pushed the idea, thought of running a single finger under the loose elastic of his shorts, feeling the scratchy pubic hair under my finger. That was a good image. No problems yet. No nausea, no disinterest, no apathetic exhaustion.

A little further mentally, then. I imagined—or maybe it was remembered—the feel of the soft, springy, warm tip of his cock against my hand, swelling in my fist as I lightly squeezed him. I pictured my hand loosely curled around his thickness, feeling the ridges and ripples and veins throbbing with life and desire and heat and seed. Mmmmm, yes. I liked that picture. This was good. I even felt my nipples harden a little as I pictured my fist sliding up and down his length. They peaked even more when I explored the memory of his body above mine, stroking deep.

I had to clamp my thighs together at that image. I thought I might have caught a whiff of my own sudden musk of desire, there and then gone, snatched away by the wind through the open window. We were approaching the outer edge of the city, suburbs becoming denser and high-rises higher.

"How long till we're at the hotel?" I asked. I may have surreptitiously tugged the neck of my sleeveless camisole down to reveal a larger expanse of cleavage.

Jeff glanced sidelong at me, then did a double take at my breasts before looking away again. "Gotta pee again already?"

I laughed and crossed my arms under my breasts, which, by this point, were nearly spilling out, my nipples hard and visible against the fabric of my shirt. "No, surprisingly. Just...antsy."

He glanced again, and his gaze lingered longer on my mostly exposed breasts. "Antsy, huh? Are you cold? Should I close the window?"

I gave him a confused look. "No, I'm fine. Why would you think I'm cold?"

He licked his lips, his gaze flickering to my breasts and then back to the road. He shifted in his seat and adjusted himself again, then gestured with a finger at my nipples. "You just look like you could cut glass there."

I waited till he glanced back at me, then tugged the shirt down to reveal one breast with a hardened, erect nipple, which I tweaked with two fingers. "They are hard, aren't they?"

Jeff groaned and leaned forward in his seat, clutching the steering wheel with both hands. "God, Anna. Put that shit away. You're teasing me, here, babe."

He leaned back again and tugged the waistband of his shorts away from his body. When he let the fabric lay against his skin once more, I saw the telltale bulge.

"Who says I'm teasing?" I asked, pulling the other side down so both breasts were bare now.

It was past midnight at this point, and the city around us was still bustling, cars passing on either side of us, street lights shedding orange glow, stoplights cycling, horns honking, steam billowing from manhole covers.

Jeff's eyes narrowed. "Anna, it's been three fucking months. Don't start something you can't finish." He glanced to either side of us, seeing cars pull parallel to us. "And put your tits away, babe. Those are mine, not for public consumption."

I laughed and tucked myself back into my bra, but left the shirt tugged down to give him a good view. "No one's consuming anything, but fine, if that's how you want it. And that's my point, Jeff: I'm starting something I *want* to finish. So get us to the hotel already."

I pulled my feet back in the car, shut the window, and leaned toward Jeff, twisting in my seat to partially face him. I settled my hand on his thigh, and he covered my hand with his, following my touch as I let my hand drift up his thigh and under the hem of his shorts.

"I'm driving as fast I can." He glanced at me as I snaked my hand into the leg of his boxers to touch bare skin, finding his shaft. "Where are you going with this, Anna?"

I shifted in my seat for better leverage. "I don't know. I just want to touch you." I gave him a long, slow stroke and smiled as he sighed, sliding down in his seat.

"God, Anna. You're making it hard to drive." He let his head flop back against the headrest.

"Want me to stop?" I clamped my fist around the tip of him, then rubbed the top of the head, smearing the sticky pre-come around him.

"Hell, no. But I also don't want to have to change in the car before checking in. And there's no way I'm letting you go down on me in the car in the middle of New York City."

I slowed my stroking of him, but didn't let go. The more I touched him like this, the more I wanted him. It felt like my libido was coming back all at once, and with a vengeance. Suddenly I found myself almost not caring if anyone saw. I was about to climb over the console and straddle him while he drove. Of course, my baby bump might get in the way, and he wouldn't be able to drive. I just held on to him, gripped him, touched him. He took corners too fast, stopped too abruptly. I grinned at his impatience, because I felt it, too. My heart pounded in my chest as I imagined his arms around me, his body hard against mine. It had been forever, for-fucking-ever. An actual eternity, it seemed. Suddenly, it felt like a lifetime had passed since I last felt him sweat into my skin, felt his breath on my neck hot and fast as he panted my name.

I slid my thighs together and tried to get closer to him, but the stupid console and my baby bump were in the way, and all I could do was touch him, feel him thick in my hands, and hope the hotel was close. Jeff glanced at the GPS in the dashboard, made a few turns, and then slowed to enter a parking garage.

"Fucking finally," he muttered, stopping and rolling his window down to take the ticket.

I had to withdraw my hand then as he searched for a parking space. He found one, jammed the truck into Park, and nearly jumped out to grab our bags from the trunk. I was slower to get out, but not by much. I smirked at Jeff as he set my suitcase down to adjust himself, his bulge clearly defined in his shorts.

"See what you do to me?" he asked, grinning.

I let my smirk fade into a sultry smile. "That's the whole idea, isn't it?" I sidled up to him, pressed my body against his, and leaned up on my tiptoes to kiss him.

His lips met mine, tasting of Coke and faintly of Doritos. He moaned softly into my mouth as I slid my tongue between his lips, then louder as I slipped my hand between us to rub him through his shorts. My belly was a hard lump between us, not in the way yet, but I realized within a few weeks, it would be. I wasn't sure how I felt about that.

A car passed by us, circling downward to a parking spot, honking as they slowed to watch us make out. Jeff pulled away, chuckling, and pushed me toward the elevator. Once we were on and the door were closed, Jeff dropped the handles to our rolling suitcases and pinned me in the corner, taking my wrists in his hands and pinioning them above my head. I tilted my head back and bared my throat to the hot, wet kisses he planted there, moving down to the hollow at the base of my throat, and farther, to the valley of my breasts.

I gasped, sighing his name, needing more than breath to feel his hands on me, his mouth on me. I felt his hardness against my thigh as he kissed my cleavage, and I reached down to grasp it in my fingers. More, I needed more. I dug my hand under his shorts to clutch him bare in my hands, relishing the hot hardness of him. I was frantic suddenly, trying to push his shorts down and my loose cotton skirt up.

And then he pulled away, leaving me limp and gasping and stunned in the corner of the elevator.

"I'm not going to fuck you in the corner of a dirty elevator, Anna," he growled, scrubbing his hand over his close-cropped scalp. "You have no idea how bad I want you right now, babe, but not like this."

I wanted to cry. A tear of absurd rejection slipped down my face. I brushed it away, irritated with myself. I was being stupid, and I knew it. Jeff was right, so right, but the sudden inrushing of my sex drive was erasing my reason.

"Anna, I—"

I shook my head, cutting him off. "No, Jeff. You're right, and I know it. I'm having one of those stupid hormonal reactions I can't exactly help." I laughed at myself through a sniffle, then tipped forward into Jeff's embrace. "Just take me to the hotel and fuck me until I can't walk."

Jeff's fingers tightened in my shoulders. "That I can do."

The elevator doors opened then, letting on a man, his wife, and three children, all chattering loudly in Arabic. Jeff and I traded glances, laughing. If Jeff hadn't stopped things when he did, this family would have gotten an eyeful.

Fifteen minutes later, we were checked in to our hotel and riding another elevator up to our floor. Jeff still had all our luggage in his hands, refusing to let me carry more than my purse. My stomach was doing flip-flops as he slid the card into the reader and pushed the door open, flipping on lights and setting our suitcases against the wall.

I hadn't gotten three steps into the room when Jeff stopped, turned in place, and wrapped a large, strong hand around my elbow, drawing me inexorably against his chest. I dropped my purse on the floor at my feet and placed my palms on his pecs, staring up into his hot brown gaze. My heart was hammering in my chest, as if this was my first time.

Except I knew what was coming, and I needed it as much as my next breath.

He didn't do anything for the space of several heartbeats, only clutched my elbow, his thumb drawing a slow circle on my skin. I stood waiting, breathing, anticipating.

Then he lifted his hand and brushed my cheek-bone with the back of his index finger, trailed the pad of his finger down my neck, across my collar-bone and down between my breasts. I sucked in a deep breath, swelling my breasts, and held it. He slipped the digit under the elastic of my camisole, pulling it down to bare one breast. I was already holding my breath, so when he touched his lips to the slope of my breast, I expelled the air in a long sigh, tipping my head back in ecstasy. He kissed down the breast to the nipple, paused to look at me, then took my nipple in his mouth and suckled it. *Oh, sweet Jesus, thank you.* Electricity shot down my body to strike at my core, sending trembles through my thighs and dampness slicking my folds.

Jeff's hand left my elbow and slid up my arm, over my shoulder, and down my back, stopping to cup my ass, drawing my hips against his. His mouth left my flesh, and he murmured, "I need you naked."

"Fuck yes," I whispered.

He pulled my camisole over my head, and my heavier-than-ever breasts fell free, bouncing and swaying. I watched in pleasure as his eyes fixed on them, revealing his desire.

Is there anything better in the world than knowing your man thinks you're beautiful? Not to me, there isn't.

He pushed my skirt off, leaving me in my panties. He liked me like that, naked except for panties. Even now, with the burgeoning roundness of my belly, he liked to kneel in front of me and take in my body, as if he were drinking in my beauty to slake an unquenchable thirst. Then he knelt forward to sit on his calves, wrapping his hands around my ankles, sliding his palms up my legs, up the back of my thighs, caressing the ever-expanding globes of my ass. He buried his face against my hip, just above the waist of my panties, kissed my skin, dug his fingers into the leg opening to stroke my wet folds. I gasped when his middle finger slid inside me, ever so slightly. I gasped again when he abruptly jerked my panties off and nudged my legs open. I spread my stance and steadied myself with my hands on his shoulders.

He swiped my folds with his tongue, clutching me close with his hands on my ass. Then, outrageously, he stopped.

"What—why are you stopping?" I demanded. "God, you can't stop now!"

He stared up at me, his brow wrinkled in confusion. "Didn't I hear somewhere that pregnant women shouldn't receive oral sex?"

I growled in my throat. "That's an old wives' tale," I said, putting my hand on the back of his head. "Just don't do a hot kitty, and we'll be fine. Now…give me orgasms." I pressed his face between my thighs and whimpered as he complied, spearing my clit with his tongue, slipping a single finger into my channel and curling it to brush me just so.

Then he stopped again. "Hot kitty?" He curled his finger once more, and my legs almost gave out.

"Blowing—blowing hot air into me." I locked my knees as he stroked inside me.

"Oh." He kissed my folds, then lapped at my opening, inciting a blissful moan from me. "That's too bad. I know you like that," he murmured, the vibrations of his voice making me shiver.

"Yeah, but just don't stop what you're doing, and I don't think I'll miss it."

He started a circular rhythm with his tongue around my swollen clit, which made my knees buckle in time with his tongue. I felt the sweet burning pressure well up within me, rising and rising with each swipe of his tongue, each curling caress of his finger. And then he added a second finger, pressing against the inner ridge, and sucked my stiffened nub into his mouth. He reached up to pinch a thick nipple between two fingers, and with that added stimulation, I exploded, falling forward against him and crying out, holding on to his shoulders for balance as my body convulsed and spasmed, heat billowing through me, lightning bursting behind my shut eyes.

He moved me back, and I felt the edge of the bed against my knees. I let myself collapse backward, gasping, feet planted on the floor. Jeff slid his body between my thighs, and I reached up, eyes still closed as aftershocks washed through me, to tug his shorts down. He peeled his T-shirt off as I took his erection in my fist and slid my hand down around his rigid, silk-soft cock. I drew him toward me, needing him, needing more of him, all of him.

"Give it to me, Jeff," I panted. "Please."

"God*damn*, Anna. You're so beautiful when you come." He leaned over me, and I felt the broad tip of his erection nudge my opening.

I pulled him closer, guided him into me. I whined in the back of my throat, a sound of pure relief, utter bliss. Jeff groaned low in his throat as he slid deep. He straightened, tucking one hand under my right knee and lifting my leg around his waist. One foot still on the floor, one around his waist, I was at the perfect height for him to stand and drive into me, his sliding shaft striking every nerve ending inside me, gliding deep, so deep, so gently and wonderfully deep.

"Oh, fuck, Anna. You don't even know how much I needed this, how much I missed this."

"I think I do."

He pulled back, almost out, then slid home again, groaning when our bodies were flush against each other. "You feel so good, Anna. Goddamn, you feel so good." He was trembling, holding back.

I fisted my hands in the blanket and lifted my hips to meet him. "More, Jeff. Harder. Please."

"I don't want to—"

I pulled at him hard with my leg, jerking him deep. "I need it, Jeff. I'm not going to break. Please, just fuck me harder."

Jeff slid out and back in, a thoughtful, hesitating thrust, then another. Then he gave me an exploratory harder thrust, and I cried out his name. That seemed to encourage him, and he pushed into me again, harder this time.

"Yes, like that," I panted. "God, that's good. More."

He rumbled in his chest. "So good." He set a fast rhythm then, and each stroke sent me further in ecstasy; each thrust had me whimpering and moaning.

And then I exploded a second time, almost out of the blue. It washed over me like a tidal wave, rolling and rollicking and detonating, and forcing a scream out of me. Jeff's hand went to my hips and pulled me hard against him. I wrapped my other leg around him, and now all that held me aloft was his arms under my ass and his shaft inside me, ramming deep in a pulsating series of short thrusts. I felt him tense, felt his buttocks clench under my legs, and knew his climax was imminent.

I clenched him with my inner muscles, clamping down as hard as I could. He groaned loudly, and I felt him release, liquid heat billowing through me, filling me. I cried out with him, not so much from my own orgasm, which was still rocking through me, but from the sheer joy of feeling Jeff come inside me, seeing the bliss on his rugged, handsome face.

I felt a second spasm rock his body, then a third smaller one, and then he was letting my legs down and pulling out of me. We crawled backward on the bed, and I curled into his side, his heart thumping under my ear, lulling me into a state of sated bliss.

As I was about to drift off to sleep, I heard him murmur, "Gonna be Caleb."

I snorted sleepily. This was an ongoing debate with us. I was sure it was a girl, but he was convinced it was a boy. So we had this argument, and it always came up just like that, as one of us was falling asleep, or on the way out the door. We each tried to get the last word in, me as he was leaving to DJ a shift, he as I was about to drift off to sleep.

I let him get the last word in, knowing I'd get him back later. Of course, the main reason I let him get away with it was that I was too sleepy to summon speech, too limp from his loving to even grunt an "uh-uh."

We still hadn't decided if we were going to find out the gender at the next ultrasound, and that was the source of a less playful debate. He wanted it to be a surprise, and I wanted to get the nursery ready with gender-appropriate decorations. Of course, Jeff was all like, "just paint it green," but that was cheating to me.

My last thought was of my own inability to decide whether I wanted it to be a girl or a boy more. I wavered from day to day. I would think of big, burly Jeff holding a little baby girl with blonde curls and Jeff's brown eyes, a big pink bow in her hair, and I'd have a mini-emotional meltdown, and then I'd picture him with a little boy who'd be the spitting image of Daddy and I'd have a different kind of breakdown, and I just couldn't decide.

I fell asleep with images of baby boys and baby girls dancing in my head. In the end, it didn't matter, because girl or boy, they'd be *ours*, and that was the only important thing.

Chapter 2: Jamie

I SLID MY PALMS FLAT OVER MY BELLY, turning sideways to look at myself in profile. My red curls were longer than they'd ever been, hanging loose nearly to my waist. They were actually kind of out of control at this point. I'd been thinking about cutting my hair for weeks now but hadn't done it. Chase would freak, for one thing. He loved my hair long. He liked to bury his fingers in it when he came inside me. If I cut it off, he'd absolutely shit his shorts.

I giggled as I pictured his reaction if I showed up at his show tonight with my hair chopped off. What if I actually, factually, shaved my head? We'd be matchers. It could be funny. Chase would probably have a heart attack. Maybe shaving my head wasn't a great plan. I took a long sheaf of springy red curls in my hand, narrowing my eyes at myself. My belly was getting ridiculous. I wasn't even twenty weeks along, and I was already getting mammoth. Stupid Anna was barely showing at all, the bitch. Here I was, big as houses, when she still could get away with most of her normal clothes. I was shopping in the maternity section already.

I sighed, smoothed my hand over my belly again, then returned to examining my hair. I held the bulk of it up at my nape, trying to picture myself with my hair at chin length. Just holding my hair up out of the way was a relief on my neck, and that was what decided me.

Time to cut my hair for the first time in my adult life. The last true haircut I'd had, not counting the odd inch or two trimmed off now and again, was before I'd moved out on my own at seventeen. I let my hair go and felt it bounce free at the small of my back, then reached for my cell phone on the bathroom counter. I got my stylist friend Lindsey to pencil me in at the last minute, called a cab, and then spent the next few minutes trying to figure out how I'd explain my sudden decision to Chase.

I'd have to seduce him, of course. As long as I left my hair long enough for him to have something to tangle his fingers in, we should be fine, I thought.

There I went, again, with the "we." I'd been referring myself in the plural lately. Myself and the baby, I guess. We. *We're gonna take a shower. We're gonna get some breakfast. We'll be fine. We're feeling nauseous.* It wasn't something I did intentionally; it just happened. It cracked Chase up to no end, which only irritated me further. I always corrected myself when I caught myself doing it, but it kept slipping out.

After putting on the sexiest bra and panties I could fit in, I put on my favorite outfit, the only thing I felt sexy in, a floor-length, high-waisted dress, scooped low in front and back to show off my ginormous preggo boobs, tucking in just right to give me some curves around my hips and ass without hugging my belly. It was ivory in color, soft against my skin, loose and comfortable, yet still let me feel attractive.

I wore it more frequently than I should, mainly because I'd never been able to find another dress like it.

The cab honked outside, and I snagged my purse and phone on the way out the door. Chase had paid a fortune for our house, but it was perfect, a brownstone walk-up in a hip but fairly quiet section of Manhattan. We had the entire first floor, and he'd let me furnish it to my heart's desire. I loved our home. I'd love it even more when his tour was over and he could stay home with me every day. His label was giving the band a couple months off, since Chase and I were having our baby, and

Gage, the bassist, claimed to need personal time. No one knew what his deal was, but Chase had made the hiatus happen since he'd noticed Gage was had been acting off lately, in a funk. I'd get Chase all to myself for six whole months before they went into the studio to start recording their first full-length album. They'd put out a couple EPs up that point, each recorded in whirlwind, marathon sessions between tour dates, but they hadn't put out anything full-length yet.

Six Foot Tall had gone viral, in a way. Someone had recorded his performance and proposal to me and uploaded it to YouTube, and it had gotten well over a million hits, which spurred the sales of their music and sold out the rest of the shows on the tour. They'd played on Leno and *Late Late Night with Jimmy Fallon*, and had been on the cover of *Rolling Stone* and *Revolver*.

All of which, of course, translated into me not having seen my husband—even after more than year, I still got giddy thinking that—in more than three months. We FaceTimed and Skyped, of course, but it wasn't the same. Skype sex wasn't anywhere near as satisfying as having Chase in my bed. Not by several orders of magnitude.

I pushed the thoughts from my mind as I sat down in Lindsey's chair and told her what I wanted, more or less. Which was, namely, shorter. Not so short Chase couldn't grab into my hair, but shorter.

Lindsey made quick work of my hair, keeping up a constant chatter in her thick New York accent, black bob nodding and ducking as she snipped and fluffed and snipped until she was satisfied. I had made her turn me around so I couldn't see myself. When Lindsey finally stepped away and tucked her scissors in her apron, I felt nerves shoot through me.

What was I thinking? Cutting my hair? Shit! Chase was going to kill me. He'd hate it. I'd hate it.

"You seriously look amazing, Jamie," Lindsey chirped, teasing my curls with her fingers before turning me around. She must have sensed my nerves. "Honest, Jamie. He'll love it, I promise. You've got to, like, trust me."

I had my hands over my eyes, refusing to look still. "What was I thinking, Linz? I don't know why I just did this, I really don't."

Lindsey laughed and took my wrists in her dainty little fingers. "You're pregnant. You know how many pregnant women I get in here who have had a sudden urge to cut their hair? It happens all the time. I'm not sure why, really, but it's a fact. It's kind of my specialty, actually. The other girls always send me the preggos, because I can usually tell when they really want to cut their hair and when they think they do but really just want it to look different. Sometimes that's all it is. Part of the nesting phase, I've heard, where you go through and, like, change everything for the baby."

I laughed. "Maybe that's it. But I don't think I'm nesting just yet. I just…wigged out, like, I all of a sudden *hated* my hair and wanted it gone, off my neck. But now? Oh, god, I'm scared to look. I haven't had it noticeably shortened in, god, like fifteen years."

Lindsey pried my hands away from my face. "Look at yourself, Jay. You're beautiful."

I sighed and opened my eyes, heart in my throat. I gasped. I looked totally different. Like, completely altered.

I interrupted my own thoughts to tell myself to stop talking like Lindsey, who, at twenty-two, had a tendency to still say "like" in every sentence.

I turned my head from side to side, marveling at how much lighter I felt. I shook my head, laughing as my hair bounced around, now hanging just above my shoulders. She'd cut away a good bit near the front so I had springs of curls as bangs that drifted across my cheekbones. It was a perfect cut for me, I realized, emphasizing my heart-shaped face and accentuating my eyes. It sharpened my jawline somehow, and brought out the curve of my throat.

Plus, there was still a good bit of hair left, so Chase could do his thing.

I pulled Lindsey into a hug, and felt my eyes prick. I cried at the drop of a hat these days. A Hallmark commercial had me bawling just the day before, and it was driving me nuts.

Lindsey pulled free and unsnapped the apron from around my neck. "So you like it?"

I nodded happily, sniffing back the traitorous tears. "I *love* it. I really do."

"And you think Chase will like it?" She grabbed a nearby broom and started sweeping up the mess of hair on the floor.

I took a deep breath. "I hope so. I think so. He'll be surprised, but once he gets over the shock, I think he'll be happy. I'll find out in a few hours, I guess."

Lindsey's gaze sharpened. "They're in town? The whole band?"

I nodded, wondering what her angle was. "Yeah, they're playing the Garden."

Lindsey crouched to brush the hair into a dustpan. "Is it sold out?"

I laughed at the hopeful tone in her voice. "Who do you have a crush on?"

Lindsey blushed, her fair skin going pink across her cheeks and on her nose. "Gage."

I nodded. "You and half the country—the half that isn't in love with my husband."

"I met him by accident the last time they played New York. He was being dragged around by some girl, a groupie, I think. She dragged him in here and got him to pay for a cut and color. I felt bad for him. She was, like, heinously obnoxious, and he was realizing it, I think. She was hot, in a bimbo sort of way. He was really nice to her, though, despite the fact that she was, like, clearly a gold-digging fame whore. He was really classy about it."

I nodded, having gotten to know Gage pretty well by that point. "That's Gage for you. He's got some rough edges, but he has a great heart, if you can get him to show you his real personality. He's got this whole hardass rocker persona that he puts on, but it's not really him."

Lindsey nodded. "I kinda got that same impression." She blushed again. "I like both sides of him."

I laughed. "The front and the back, you mean?"

Lindsey turned red. "That's not what I meant!"

I elbowed her playfully. "Sure it's not. You know you were checking out his ass."

She rolled her eyes, then leaned in to whisper to me. "Actually, he *was* wearing these tight, ripped jeans that hugged him, like, *all* over. I couldn't stop staring at him." She dropped her voice to almost inaudible. "He sat so I had this crazy crotch-shot of him, and I swear, I nearly cut a chunk out of his bimbo friend's ear because I was staring at his bulge the whole time."

I laughed so hard I snorted. "Would've served her right. But, while he's not my husband, Gage is pretty hot."

"Yeah, he is," she muttered, her tone wistful.

I waited for her to ask, but after a few moments, it became clear she wasn't going to. "You want to come with me?"

She looked up, hope gleaming in her eyes. "Oh, god, really? You have an extra ticket?"

I laughed. "I'm married to the lead singer, honey. I don't need tickets. I've got a box wherever he's playing. He made sure of it."

"That's the coolest thing ever." She clapped her hands. "I get off in an hour, and now that's gonna be the longest hour of my life!"

I stood up slowly and walked with her to the register. "You know where I live, right? Drop by when you're done, and we'll go early to see the guys."

As I left, Lindsey hugged me and thanked me about fifty times, and refused to let me pay her for the cut. I laughed as I hailed a cab, watching her pull out her phone and text furiously. I don't think I'd ever seen anyone so excited in all my life. Maybe she could pull Gage out of whatever funk he was lost in.

I ate a quick dinner at a bistro near Lindsey's salon and then went to my standing weekly mani-pedi appointment. About a week after we got back from our honeymoon, Chase had insisted I make the appointment and set it for every week. He claimed I'd been beans-and-ricing it for too long, and it was time to let him take care of me. Apparently, now that money was rolling in for the band, that meant all sorts of lavish treatment I'd never imagined would be a part of my life, such as standing manicure appointments, shopping trips to Fifth Avenue, and even a car and driver if I wanted it. I'd drawn the line at being chauffeured. Chase was quickly becoming a rock star and a household name, and that meant lots of money, but I'd lived a relatively simple life, taking care of myself and using the occasional indulgence as a treat for meeting my responsibilities. I couldn't take the swing in the complete opposite direction, not all at once at least. A new purse whenever I wanted it? Awesome. Louboutin pumps and Chanel pajamas? Hell, yes. Pretending like I'm some swanky celebrity, with an entourage and a driver and bodyguards everywhere I go? Hell, no. I may be married to a rock star, but I'm still Jamie Dunleavy—Jamie Delany, now—and I'm no poser.

Lindsey was *click-clicking* up the sidewalk toward my house as I was stepping out of the cab. I had to stifle a smile and a giggle, as she'd kind of overdone it in her excitement. She was wearing a miniskirt that only barely covered her tiny little ass, and a tight-fitting, low-cut sleeveless shirt that very blatantly accentuated her decent-sized tatas—and by accentuated, I mean pushed up to overflowing. She was also wearing a pair of four-inch spike heels that were ridiculously impractical for a rock concert.

"Wow, Linz," I said, eyeing her outfit skeptically, "You're really...going all out, huh?"

She grinned. "Yep."

"Well, there's no way Gage could possibly resist you in that outfit," I said.

She ducked her head. "That's the point, isn't it?"

I poured Lindsey a glass of wine and wished I could have some myself. Yeah, the doctor had said half a glass every once in a while was fine, but I knew myself, and I knew there was no point to drinking half a glass of wine. Half a glass of wine was like being brought to the edge of orgasm and then abandoned.

I regretted my analogy as soon as it passed through my head: I hadn't seen Chase in three months. Which meant I hadn't had an orgasm in three months. I'd tried, of course. We'd Skyped and tried getting a little nasty that way, but it just fell flat for both of us. My own fingers were useless now that I'd become addicted to Chase's. Even my vibrator hadn't gotten me anywhere. And now I was mere hours from getting what I so desperately needed, namely, an exhausting marathon session of fucking Chase's brains out, followed by some epic cuddling.

I shivered in anticipation even as I thought about it. I felt my nipples tighten and my panties dampen just picturing Chase above me, naked, sweaty, and mine.

"Come on, Linz," I said, "I can't wait anymore. I need Chase."

Lindsey laughed and tossed back the last two swallows of wine. "I'm ready."

A cab was letting out my neighbor as we stepped out of the brownstone, and we climbed in, exchanging hugs with Mrs. Lettis as we passed. Mrs. Lettis was a hugger. She hugged everyone and anyone. When Chase and I had first come to look at the brownstone, she'd shown up to chatter about the previous tenants, and Chase and I hadn't been able to get away without at least three hugs each from the sweet, elderly, buxom woman.

Linz giggled as the cab pulled away from the curb. "She's…nice."

"She really is. I once watched her hug a drug dealer. Seriously. I walked her to the store once, and this guy was in the freezer section, buying ice cream. He stank of weed and paid for his ice cream from a roll of hundreds so thick he needed an industrial-size rubber band." I scrolled through my Facebook newsfeed on my phone as I spoke. "Well, this guy had all this cash, but the cashier didn't have enough correct change to give him back, since the dealer only had hundred-dollar bills. This was at, like, eight in the morning. So Mrs. Lettis, being the kind of woman she is, paid for the guy's ice cream. Now you have to understand, this guy was *scary*. Tattoos all up and down his arms and on his throat, pierced lip, ears, and nose, arms bigger around than your waist, 'thug life' tattooed across his knuckles. Mrs. Lettis paid for his ice cream without batting an eyelash at him. He was stunned, like, speechless. He tried to thank her and pay her back, and she just clucked at him, and leaned in to give him a hug. He just stood there, frozen, like, 'what the fuck do I do?' God, Linz, it was *so* funny. She patted his face and said, 'everyone needs ice cream, dear.' The cashier, who'd been pissing himself, couldn't believe it."

Linz giggled. "She sounds awesome."

"You have no clue. I'm pretty sure that dealer visits her every week, like, staking out his turf so no one messes with her. It's cute."

The cab dropped us off at the gate, where I showed the security my backstage pass and we were waved through. Linz stuck close to me as we wove our way through the bustle of techies, roadies, band members, and all the other assorted people necessary to make a concert happen. It was huge show, with Six Foot Tall being only one of the headlining bands, along with Theory of a Dead Man, Drowning Pool, and System of a Down. There were also almost half a dozen opening bands, a mix of local talent and up-and-coming acts. Needless to say, finding my husband in the chaos proved to be nearly impossible. The back-stage area was huge and crowded, everyone scurrying and chattering into walkie-talkies, checking lists on tablets as they walked. We found Gage first, sitting on a black box that once held sound equipment of some kind, restringing his bass. He glanced up as we approached, and his face lit up, hazel eyes bright. He ran a hand through his long, loose, pale blond hair, his massive bicep flexing with the motion. Gage was huge, standing at least six-four and weighing a good two-fifty in solid muscle. He was an MMA fighter before he joined the band with Chase, and it showed in the rugged, scarred features of his face, which, despite the roughness, were still handsome in a Dolph Lundgren sort of way.

"'Sup, Jay." He stood up and gave me a one-armed hug, resting his bass on the toe of his Timberland boot. "Who's your tasty-looking friend?" His eyes took on an avid, hungry gleam.

I heard Lindsey suck in a surprised gasp at Gage's words, but she recovered quickly. "I'm Lindsey," she breathed, sticking her hand out.

Gage took her hand in his, but instead of shaking it, he used it to pull her closer. "I'm Gage."

Lindsey stood with barely an inch separating her from Gage, each breath she took swelling her breasts to touch Gage's chest. "I know," she said. "I cut your girlfriend's hair the last time you guys were here."

Gage frowned, struggling to remember. Then his face cleared, and he guffawed in laughter. "She was not my girlfriend. I didn't even bang her. She was too fucking obnoxious. She was a fucking slut, and, coming from me, that's saying something."

Lindsey snorted. "She only wanted to be near you 'cause you're famous."

Gage nodded, and then his gaze sharpened. "And you? Why do want to be near me?"

"Because I think I could like you."

Good answer, Linz, I thought. I passed behind Lindsey and fixed Gage with a hard stare, telling him without words that if he hurt my friend, I'd have his balls. He smirked and nodded subtly, letting me know he heard my unspoken message.

I heard the telltale *rat-a-tat-tat* of Johnny Hawk, the drummer, tapping his sticks against a counter, and the click of a pick hitting the strings of an un-amped guitar. I found the door, peeked my head in and said my hellos to Johnny and Kyle, and asked if they knew where Chase was.

"He's by the stage, I think," Kyle said, tweaking the tuning of his guitar without looking up at me. When he had the tuning right, he looked up at me with a bright smile, which morphed into a surprised expression. "Damn, Jay. You got *really* pregnant."

I gave him the finger and a nasty glare. "Smooth, Kyle. Real smooth. What you meant to say is, 'damn, Jay, you're huge.'"

Johnny, the youngest of the band at barely twenty-three, made an *oh, shit* face, which made me laugh. Kyle held up a hand in a gesture of surrender. "No! That's not—I just meant..." He sighed in exasperation. "Damn, you pregnant chicks are touchy. You look good, Jay. You really do."

I grinned at him. "I'm just giving you shit, Kyle. But don't say that to any other pregnant lady. You'll get your block knocked off."

I left the room then and went toward the stage in search of Chase. I heard his voice before I saw him, and he sounded irritated.

"This isn't the time or place, Jenna. And I'm not the guy. I'm married. You know that."

A whiny female voice, breathy with overt seduction, responded. "Oh, come on, Chase. It doesn't have to be like that. You know you want to. You've been such a good boy all tour, don't you think you deserve a little treat?"

I felt rage boil through me. Who was this bitch trying to seduce my husband? I tried to take a few calming breaths, but it wasn't working. My Irish temper was up and hotter than was safe. I felt my hands clench into fists, and before I knew it, I was rounding the corner to the dead-end emergency exit hallway.

What I saw had me even angrier. The groupie, Jenna, was on her knees and crawling toward Chase, who was backing away from her, toward me. She had his belt in her hands, and had clearly fallen to her knees to try to go down on him, but had only managed to snag his belt off him before he got away.

The little bitch saw me at that moment and paled, scrambling to her feet and dropping the belt. Chase spun in place, eyes flying wide.

"Jamie!" He took a step toward me, and I held out my hand to stop him. He halted, sucking in a harsh breath. "I didn't do anything, Jay! I swear!"

"I saw everything, baby." I cut my eyes at him, let them soften so he'd know I wasn't mad at him. I then fixed my glare on the groupie. "You. What the *fuck* do you think you're doing?"

"I—I—I'm sorry, Jamie, I mean, Mrs. Delany. I just, I wanted—" She shook her head, bleached hair flying.

Mrs. Delany, I thought. *I like the sound of that.*

"You wanted a piece of Chase," I said, my voice deceptively calm. "I can understand that. He's a hot piece of man. But the problem here is that he's *my* husband."

She took a step backward, away from me, as I stalked closer. "I know, I'm sorry—"

I was within striking distance now, but I wanted to make my point first. "That's right, you are sorry. You're a sorry piece-of-shit whore." I was caught up in the rage now. I knew should stop, but I couldn't. "He's my *husband*, you cunt. Stay the *fuck* away from him."

She was trembling now, but anger and panic were replacing fear. "Listen, bitch, I said I'm sorry. Now move—" She didn't get the chance to finish her statement.

My fist cracked against her nose, breaking it in a spray of blood. My hand immediately went numb and then began radiating pain as my knuckles absorbed the force of the blow. The groupie dropped to the ground, screaming. I heard a muffled laugh behind me and turned in place, shaking my hand, to see the whole band watching. They were all laughing, shoulders quivering in mirth, fists covering their mouths as they cackled.

"That was fucking *epic*!" Johnny yelled, doubled over, hooting.

I grinned as the other guys clustered around me, patting me on the back and chattering all at once. The laughter abated as a black T-shirted security guy pushed between us, lifted Jenna by the arms to her feet, and shoved her, just this side of too rough, toward the exit. As they rounded the corner, she leveled an evil glare at me, the entire lower half of her face a wash of blood, her huge fake tits coated in red.

Chase stepped in front of me, took my hand in his, and rubbed my knuckles with a gentle thumb. "You okay?"

I nodded, stepping closer to him so our bodies were flush, my belly and breasts crushed against him. "I can't believe her. Does she do shit like that often?"

Chase tilted his head back and groaned. "Unfortunately, yeah. She's the sister of one of the roadies, and she's always around. I'm pretty sure ninety percent of the guys on the tour have fucked her at least once. They kind of pass her around. It's gross."

I spared a glance at the other guys from the band. "None of you have fucked her, have you?"

Gage and Kyle both made disgusted grimaces and shook their heads. Johnny, however, looked embarrassed.

"Johnny!" I yelled. "Tell me you didn't. That's fucking nasty! She's gotta have more diseases than a cockroach!"

He shrugged. "I didn't sleep with her, I just— she…she gave me a BJ once." He turned eight shades of red, tugging on the end of his long, braided black goatee.

Gage shoved him, hard enough that Johnny slammed into the wall opposite. "Stay away from that bitch, Johnny. She's a ho. She's poisonous, man. She'll fuck anything with a cock, and she'll do anything to get what she wants."

"Well, she's *not* getting my man," I growled, and the guys all laughed. "You think it's funny now, but it won't be so funny when I go to jail for assault and battery."

Chase took my face in his hands, and his mocha-brown eyes delved into mine. "You have nothing to worry about, baby. There's only you."

I kissed his hard, stubble-rough jaw. "I know. I trust you. It's other women I don't trust."

Chase turned his face down so his mouth met my next kiss. "That was hot, Jay. Seriously. I like you when you're possessive."

I let the heat of my desire blaze in my eyes as I looked up at him. "You're *mine*, Chase."

I heard Gage clear his throat. "Let's go, guys. I think it's about to get hot in hurrr." He slurred the last word as a play on the hip-hop/pop song from a few years ago.

Chase chuckled against my mouth, then cupped my ass with his hands to pull me tighter against his body. "It's gettin' hot in hurr, so take off all your clothes," he murmured, slipping his hands over the bare skin of my back where the back of the dress dipped down.

"Find me room with a lock, and I will," I said, dragging my fingernails down the back of his faded, tattered, black *Return of the Jedi* T-shirt.

His fingers clawed into the soft flesh and firm muscle of my backside, then released me. "Wait a second...goddamn, Jay, what happened to your hair?" He ran his fingers through it, fluffing it, tangling his hands into the shortened curls.

"Took you long enough to notice," I said. "Do you like it?"

Chase stepped back and scrutinized me. "It's different."

My heart palpitated crazily. "That doesn't sound good."

"No! I just—I have to get used to it. You cut a *lot* off, baby. It's a shock. I didn't notice before because of the excitement, but now that I'm really looking at you...I like it. I do."

I narrowed my eyes at him. "Liar. You hate it." I turned away, feeling my heart clench. It was just hair, I knew, and it would grow back, but...the thought of Chase not being attracted to me had me sick to my stomach.

I stormed past him, but I didn't get three feet before his arm wrapped around my waist and pulled me back against him. My breath caught at the familiar feel of his body against mine, the power in his hands as they smoothed down my hips, the heat of his breath on my neck, now bare and open to his mouth. His palm skated over my belly, briefly tender and loving, and then skimmed up to cup my breast, his thumb nudging the edge down to bare more skin, then yet more, digging down until one nipple was peeking out. I felt my thighs clench as desire rocketed through me. His erection was a hard, thick rod against the top of my buttocks and the small of my back.

He ground his hips against me, pressing his shaft into me. "Feel that?" His voice was a low rumble in my ear. "Does that feel like I hate it? You just surprised me is all, baby. I love it. Now I can kiss your shoulders, just...like...this..." He suited action to words, planting hot kisses along my shoulder blade and up my neck between each word.

I shivered under his mouth, pressed my thighs together, needing pressure; one of Chase's hands— not the one thumbing light circles over the tip of my nipple—slid down my side to my hip, bunching in the cotton where my hip dipped in to my thigh, and brushed the "V" where I so desperately needed his touch. In that moment, I didn't care where we were, who could round the corner and see.

Chase walked forward with me, never breaking contact or pausing in his kissing of my skin, now behind my ear, beneath it, over my jawline and to my chin. He found a doorknob, twisted it, pushed it open. We startled a group of men in the act of snorting lines of cocaine, three roadies by the look of them, and one guy who looked like a rocker, with spiked dyed red hair and spike-studded leather bracelets on his wrists.

"Out," Chase growled.

The rocker drew a short straw along the last line, blinked hard as he sniffed. The guys stood lazily, one of them brushing his forearm over the low table they'd been snorting from. The rocker was the last one out the door, and he threw a lecherous glance over his shoulder. "Fuck her good, mate," he said, his voice thick with a British accent.

"She's my wife, asshole," Chase said, shooting a hard glare at the man.

The British rocker just smirked as he sauntered off, not bothering to reply, pulling a guitar pick from his back pocket.

Chase pushed the door closed and twisted the lock, then turned to me. "Sorry about them."

I shrugged. "It's a concert—they're rock stars. What do you expect?"

Chase pulled a face. "I just hate that shit. Coke, I mean. When Gage and I started the band, we made a pact that we'd never do drugs, and that no one who played with us would, either. We actually fired our first drummer for that same thing, not long before I met Anna. We caught him doing lines off a stripper's tits in the back room of a nightclub when he was supposed to be with us, practicing."

"I knew people who did it regularly. I never liked it. I tried it once, but I hated it. Plus, I watched too many friends fuck up their lives using it."

Chase nodded. "A buddy of mine OD'd. Right in front of me. I watched him go, and I couldn't stop it."

His eyes darkened and narrowed with memory. I closed the distance between us, pushing my breasts up against him and running my fingers up under his shirt.

"Hey," I said, tilting my face up for a kiss, "enough of that. Where were we?"

Chase shook his head to clear it, and when his eyes descended to mine, they were hot with lust once more. "God, I missed you. Do you have any idea? If I didn't love performing so much, I'd quit because I just can't stand being away from you so much."

"I'd never let you quit," I said. "It's what you do, part of who you are. I miss you, too, more than you know, but it just makes these reunions that much better."

He grinned at me, and the sight of his smile still had the power to take my breath away. Then he kissed me, and my breath was truly snatched, sucked away by the desperation of his mouth moving on mine. I melted into him, slid my palms up under his shirt and clawed my nails down his spine, feeling tingles begin in my core. Chase curled his fingers into the fabric of my dress at my hips, gathering the material into his hands to slowly bare my legs. The anticipation of his hands on my flesh caused me to shiver all over, to lean up on my toes to deepen the kiss. I put every shred of my desire, my need, my three months' worth of pent-up sexual frustration into the kiss. At some point I pushed his shirt off so I could roam my hands over his rock-hard, sculpted torso, and then I was fumbling with his belt and zipper and button, pushing his boxers away as well.

And then—god, yes—he was naked for me, right there in the office or whatever this room was. Hard for me. So hard, so huge. Thick and pink and veined and ridged and rippled, and begging for my touch. I trailed my fingers slowly down his stomach, nibbling on his lower lip. Chase sucked his belly in, still slowly gathering my dress up at my hips. I loved this teasing, this give and take. Chase blew out a sigh of ultimate pleasure and relief as I finally wrapped my hand around his cock, and when he did, I smiled at him, my lips curving against the line of his jaw.

"God, Jay. God, I love your hand on me."

"You like that?" I teased. "You want more?"

He bucked his hips into my plunging fist. "Yes, *fuck* yes."

"Then touch me." I straddled his knee, clenching my thighs around his leg and rubbing myself against him.

Chase waited a beat, then peeled my dress off over my head and tossed it aside. He pushed me back a few inches and took in my body, and his eyes went heavy-lidded with appreciation. "God, Jay. You're...you are honestly the sexiest goddamn woman in the world. You're heaven, my love. Absolute perfection."

Again with the prickling eyes. I reached up behind me to unclasp my bra, letting it fall away so Chase could gaze at me. He closed the gap slowly, cupping my bare breasts in his big, hard, callused hands, gently massaging them. He knew by now that they were sensitive, so he was extra gentle. Of course, I'd gotten three months more pregnant since he'd seen me last, and now they were even more sensitive. Just the ever-so-slight brush of his palms over my nipples had me wet and shivering, gasping. And then he bent and pulled me to him, lowering his mouth over my breast and suckling a rigid nipple between his lips. I cried out against his shoulder, and then full-on bit him when he slipped his fingers between my thighs, cupping me over my panties.

I had his erection in my fist again, sliding my fingers around him, rubbing the tip with my thumb, squeezing low on the base the way he liked it, pulsing my fist around him in short squeezes as I slicked his pre-come over him. His thumb hooked over my panties and jerked them down, and I stepped out, widening my stance, and then whimpered into his bicep when he slipped two thick fingers into my wet, arousal-pungent folds.

"I need you, baby," I said. "Now. Take me now."

Chase laughed, almost mockingly. His fingers curled inside me, eliciting a muffled shriek, and then his thumb pressed over my ultra-sensitive clit, and I was undone. I latched my teeth onto the round of his shoulder and let myself scream as I came apart.

"Goddamn, Jay. You came fast." Chase didn't relent when I came, but curled his fingers inside me again, and I had no choice but to ride his hand, rubbing against him and whimpering, crying out. My orgasm hadn't slowed, hadn't abated, and when he slid to his knees in front of me, I let my head fall back and steadied myself on his broad shoulders, knowing I was about to be ripped in two by his talented tongue.

His tongue stroked up my crease, and I shivered, shook, trembled, aftershocks hitting me with sledgehammer force even as another orgasm built up within me. The tip of his tongue touched my clit, lightly, and then circled it. I moaned long and low, the sound rising in pitch until I was keening in my throat, dipping with my knees at each curling lap of his tongue in me. I rode his face, arched my back, and fucked his tongue with my folds, greedily gorging myself on the high. I cried out his name as the third orgasm punched through me, leaving me breathless and limp.

Chase chose that moment, the instant of utter satiety and complete bonelessness, to move behind me and spin me in place. He lifted my foot and placed it on the low coffee table, which was pushed up against the wall. I bent forward, planting my palms on the wall and braced myself, waiting.

He took his time. He slid up against me, dragging the tip of his cock along my thigh, nudging my folds. I gasped at the presence of him there, held my breath, tensed and waiting, needing it. He pushed against me, and I whined when he moved away.

"I need you inside me, Chase." I could barely gasp the words.

He mouthed my neck in the hollow between shoulder and throat, cupping my breasts with both hands. He put his foot next to mine, nestled his tip in my folds. I arched my back, silently begging him. I heard him suck in a breath, and then he was sliding up, sliding in, and I sobbed in relief, in desperate ecstasy. I heard him moan, felt the vibrations of his voice on my skin. I held my breath and waited, every muscle tensed, my heart hammering absurdly in my chest.

And then he was inside me, sweet and deep and slowly pushing deeper. I let out my tension in a gasp, sinking down to meet him. He lifted up on his toes to drive himself deeper, swiveling his hips in a circle as he reached full impalement. I draped myself against the wall, head down, watching his hands cup and caress my breasts. His right hand slithered down my belly and between my thighs, and then his fingers curled in to slide against my clit, and I screamed into my forearm, biting it until pain laced the pleasure. I grabbed Chase's thigh and pulled him, urging him harder, faster, but he resisted. He lowered himself from his tiptoes and onto flat feet, then pulled his hips away until he was nearly out of me and I was whimpering with the loss of him within me. He held there, circling my clit with his fingers, then began pulsating his hips so his tip slipped shallowly in and out between my swollen labia.

"Oh fuck, baby," I moaned, "stop teasing me. Give me all of you."

He clutched my breast in one hand, pressed his fingers against my nerve endings with the other, hesitated for a beat like that, then thrust hard into me. Once, twice, three times, hard and arrhythmic, and then he was gasping against my neck and pumping his cock into me, fast and hard and so perfect.

"Like that?" he asked, rolling my nipple in his fingers.

"Yes, yes…like this. Don't stop." I clutched his thigh in my hand and pulled him closer, arched my back and lowered my hips into his frantic thrusting.

I came a fourth time, a nuclear detonation within me, my inner muscles clamping down around his thick, slick, sliding shaft, my breath stopped and gasping in stutters, heart palpitating, fire and heat and lightning shuddering through every fiber of my body.

I knew, in that moment, what Chase needed. I knew he was close, and I knew how he liked to come. I pushed away from the wall, lifted up to pull him out of me, ignoring his curse of protest. He followed me to the floor as I settled on my knees and forearms, presenting my ass to him. I was quivering all over, aftershocks crashing in my muscles and my core, but I held the pose, watching him over my shoulder. He grinned, licked his lips dramatically, and settled on his knees behind me. He grabbed himself at the base, feathered his fingers into my slick folds, and guided himself in, sliding deep.

"Oh, fuck, Jamie. God you're perfect. So tight." He grabbed my leg at the quadricep and lifted so my thigh was resting on his outstretched knee, and I nearly collapsed at how deep he went, how he struck every sensitive place inside me from the angle of his penetration. "I've dreamt of being inside you like this every night for three months."

"Me, too," I gasped.

I didn't think I would, or could, come again, but when he started shifting his hips to drive into me deep and slow, I felt it rising again. Impossible. I almost feared how hard I would climax if he took me over the edge a fifth time. Five times in thirty minutes? I'd be a puddly mess.

But I did. As Chase began to groan and grunt with each staccato thrust, I felt it rip through me. "Chase, baby…come with me. Right now."

He thrust hard into me, and I felt him unleash within me, filling me, and his voice filled the room with a long, low growl. I didn't scream, didn't cry out or whimper; I was left too breathless by the potency of my climax. I could only clench my fists and open my mouth wide in a silent scream, rocked forward by his crashing hips. And then he was limp behind me, his cheek resting on my back and his cock softening within me.

"Holy shit, baby," I said, collapsing onto my belly on the floor. "That was…incredible."

Chase flopped to his back next to me. "Yeah, it was." He twisted onto his side to smirk at me. "That was just the beginning, babe. You have no idea what I'm going to do to you tonight after the show. You won't be able to walk tomorrow."

I rolled to my back and pulled him over me. "I already won't be able to. You just ruined me. I'm done."

Chase lowered his lips to mine, kissing me with a sweetness that belied the ferocity of our lovemaking from just moments ago. "I wasn't too rough, was I?"

I held him by the nape and met his gaze. "No, baby. You were perfect. Exactly what I needed, just like you always are. You won't hurt me, or the baby." I squirmed beneath him. "You did make me all drippy, though. I think you came an entire gallon."

He laughed. "I had a lot built up."

I scrutinized his face. "You didn't take care of yourself at all?"

He shrugged, rolling off me. "Once, about two weeks after I left. It sucked. It's just not the same, not satisfying at all. I'd rather have blue balls and wait until I can be with you." He extended his hand to me and lifted me to my feet.

I put on my bra and slipped the dress over my head, stuffing my panties into my purse.

"Not gonna put those back on?" Chase asked as he dressed.

I shook my head. "No, not until I can go to the bathroom and clean up. I don't think you understand how much you came, Chase. Even after I clean up, I'll be dripping for days."

He tied his boot and stood up, pulling me against him. "Sorry. I didn't think to bring a condom."

I shrugged and scrubbed my palm over his shaved head. "It's fine. I like feeling you bare inside me. I'll just be...squishy for a while." I rubbed his head again, then looked into his eyes. "You should grow your hair back. I'm tired of bald Chase."

He smirked at me. "Fine, if you want me to."

At that moment someone knocked on the door. "Sorry, guys, but we gotta be on in ten," Gage said.

"Coming right now," Chase said.

I snickered. "You already did," I said.

"Whoa, TMI, guys," Gage said, laughing.

Chase kissed me, long and slow, and then we exited the room. Gage gave us a knowing smirk as I ran my fingers through my hair, which very likely looked as thoroughly just-fucked as I was in all actuality. I walked with Gage and Chase, chatting about the other bands on the tour.

They escorted me to the hallway, and I glanced at Gage. "Where's Lindsey?" I asked.

"In the box already."

"You better be nice to her, Gage Gallagher," I warned. "She's a sweet girl, not one of your groupie sluts. Don't hurt her."

Gage met my gaze, his eyes serious. "I know, Jay. I won't, I promise. I'm taking her on a for-real date after the show."

I gave him a surprised look, as I'd never known Gage to take a girl on a date before. He was in many ways a stereotypical rock star, especially when it came to women.

Before we parted ways, I pulled Chase aside. "Will you be here for the ultrasound on Thursday?" I tried to sound casual, and didn't entirely succeed.

I would never tell him how much I wanted him there. If he couldn't make it, it wouldn't be his fault, and I knew it. I'd been putting off asking him until I saw him in person, and I wanted to keep putting it off, because I knew what the answer would likely be. I held my breath as he considered.

"I honestly don't know, babe," Chase said, grimacing. "I really want to be there. All I can promise you at this moment is that I will do everything in my power to be there."

I swallowed, hard. "That's all I'm asking. Do your best."

Chase's eyes found mine, and they were piercing. "What aren't you saying?"

I shook my head and brushed a wayward red curl out of my mouth. "Nothing, honey. It's just... I'm really hoping you'll be there." I put my hand over his mouth before he could speak. "I know you can't promise me. And if you can't, that's how it is. I knew there'd be the risk of this kind of thing when I married you. Just try, okay? Now go kill 'em." I leaned in, kissed him, and then turned him around by his shoulders and pushed him away, smacking his ass as he went.

I made my way to the private box and slid into my seat next to Lindsey, who was, as usual, busily tapping away at her phone.

She looked up when I appeared, and grinned at me. "Well, well, well," she said, "don't you look pleased with yourself."

I rolled my eyes at her. "More like pleased with my husband," I said, covering up my inner turmoil over the upcoming ultrasound appointment. "So I hear Gage is taking you out later."

Lindsey blushed. "Yeah, I wasn't expecting that. I mean, he's Gage Gallagher. He's got a reputation already, and they've only been a big deal for, like, a year." She picked at a thread on the hem of her miniskirt. "I'm kinda nervous."

I patted her knee. "You should be, hon. Gage is a force of nature. The fact that he's taking you on an actual date? That's huge, Linz. He likes you."

She narrowed her eyes at me. "Did you say something to him?"

I shrugged and accepted a diet Coke from the server. "I might have told him I'd cut off his balls if he hurt you. No big deal. Not like he could possibly mistake you for one, but I just didn't want him to treat you like one of his little groupie hookers. You're a classy chick, and he needs to treat you like one." I turned a serious look at her. "If he doesn't treat you right, ditch his ass. Just 'cause he's a rock star doesn't mean he can treat you like shit."

Lindsey frowned at me. "I appreciate your intentions, Jay. But I think I know what I'm getting myself into."

I laughed. "You don't know Gage if that's what you think."

Lindsey turned to the stage as the lights went down, and I caught a thoughtful expression on her face before the stadium went dark. I wasn't about to tell Lindsey some of the things I knew about Gage, none of them bad, per se. He was an intense person, and not someone to lightly enter into any kind of a relationship with, rock star status aside. I wondered if Lindsey really had any clue what she was in for.

Those thoughts were erased as a spotlight bathed each band member, Chase in front, right at the edge of the stage, Gage and Kyle to either side, and Johnny in the middle on his elaborate drum set. The crowd went wild for several moments, screaming and clapping, then gradually faded into silence as the band merely stood in place—or sat, in Johnny's case—waiting. When the silence was complete, Johnny hit the kick drum in a slow rhythm, *bang...bang...bang...* building anticipation, getting blood boiling. The beat gave nothing away as to which song they'd start off with, and the crowd became restless as the kick drum rhythm continued, drawing out the tension. Chase extended his hand out to the side, low, and then slowly raised it. For every few inches Chase raised his arm, Johnny increased the tempo of his kick drum, until Chase's hand was vertical over his head and Johnny was kicking the pedal faster than I'd thought possible. They held this for a heartbeat, and then Chase dropped his hand in downward slice. The gesture cut Gage and Kyle loose, and they both cut into a blistering power riff, the stage lights bursting into a flashing pattern. Chase bobbed his head in time to the music, then slowly brought the mic to his mouth and began the intro hook to one of their hardest numbers, a piece Chase told me was a tribute to Slipknot, Gage's favorite band.

I watched them perform, watched my husband work the crowd into a frenzy, bringing them in on the crowd-favorite numbers, jumping out into the front rows of the mosh pit at one point, which had my heart in my throat until the security men had him safely onstage once more.

I wasn't really into the show, though. Not all the way. My mind was on the ultrasound, and whether I really had what it took to be the wife of a rock star when it came time to have the baby. If I went into labor early, would he be able to get there in time? Would he be around for the baby's first smile, first word, first step? Every once in a while I'd catch a pensive look on Chase's face, and I knew he had the same concerns.

It was the day of the ultrasound, and I'd been fighting tears all day. Chase had called me the day before to tell me he had an interview today and wouldn't be at the appointment. I knew it was silly. I knew it was just an ultrasound. At least, that was what I told myself to keep myself calm. He'd be here if he could.

Right? It was hard not to question everything, with the way my emotions were running rampant.

I sat in the waiting room, reading through old text conversations between Chase and me, just to feel any kind of a connection with him. My heart was in my throat, my eyes burning.

A nurse in maroon scrubs called my name, and I followed her down a short hallway, where she weighed me, and then ushered me into a dimly lit room. I slid onto the elevated chair, my phone clutched in my fist, waiting for the technician.

My phone buzzed in my hand and I slid the green icon across the "lock" screen to open the thread.

You have wifi access right now?

I went through the requisite steps to access the guest wifi for the doctor's office, and then texted him back. *Yep. Why?*

The three dots in a gray bubble appeared, and his response came through a few seconds later. *I put the interview on hold until after your appointment. FaceTime me.*

I put my hand over my mouth and held back a sob. He'd found a way to be here anyway. I sucked in a deep breath to calm myself, hating how emotional I was all the time. I'd never been the kind of girl to cry at every little thing, so this was especially frustrating, since I couldn't stop it. The technician came in and sat down in her chair, greeting me. She was a thin, younger woman with black hair cut in a short bob, and she had the coldest hands I'd ever felt.

The nurse tapped at the keyboard, slid my shirt up, and lined the waistband of my yoga pants with a white towel before slathering the frigid blue goo on my belly.

"Is it okay if I have my husband on the phone with me for this?" I asked her. "He couldn't be here for the appointment, but he wants to be involved."

"Sure," the technician responded without looking away from her screen.

I tapped the *FaceTime* button on my phone, and after a few rings, Chase's face appeared on the screen of my iPhone. I smiled at him, and we talked about the upcoming interview for Spin. When the nurse began sliding the wand across my stomach, Chase asked me to show him what was going on. I turned the phone around and showed him to the nurse, who flashed him a distracted and slightly irritated smile, which turned to awe when she realized who he was. I showed him the ultrasound equipment, and then focused on the screen showing the baby.

The nurse hit a key, and the room was filled with the distorted *thumpthump—thumpthump* of the heartbeat, and Chase gave a choked laugh at the sound.

"Is that the heartbeat?" he asked.

"Yes," the nurse replied. "And it's a good one. Right in the middle of the best range. I'm gonna see if I can get a good shot at the gender now."

I swiveled the phone so I could see Chase, and felt love for him ripple through me at the emotions I saw written on his features.

"Where are you?" I asked him.

"I'm in the hotel room in Columbus," he replied. "The guys are all down in the conference room, waiting for the interview to start."

"Oh, here, look!" The nurse pointed at the screen, holding the wand low on my belly at an angle.

I turned the phone so Chase could see the monitor clearly. There was a blob of white against grainy black, moving and shimmering as the baby wiggled inside me. I couldn't make anything out at first, but then I realized what I was seeing.

"It's a girl, Chase, you see it?" My throat was thick as I spoke, and I mentally cursed the damned emotions.

"I see, baby. I see. It's a girl. Our daughter." He was equally as emotional, so I didn't feel as embarrassed by my own.

I turned the phone back to me, seeing a single tear streak down Chase's face. "God*damn* it, Jay. I wish I was there with you. We're having a daughter. A baby girl." He wiped his face and forced a laugh out. "It didn't seem really real until now, you know? Seeing it there on the screen made it...god. Fuck, I'm really going to be a father." He scrubbed his palm over his scalp, which was now darkened by growing hair.

"I know what you mean," I said. "I knew it was real because I'm the one with the baby growing inside me, but this makes it all the more real."

"Do you guys have a name picked out?" the nurse asked.

"We've discussed a few," I said. "He likes Beth, and I like Samantha, after my grandmother. We haven't decided yet."

"Actually," Chase cut in, "I've been thinking, and I want to go with Samantha. Sam."

I looked at him in surprise, seeing the satisfaction cross his face. "Are you sure?"

"Yeah, I'm sure." He smiled at me, and I wished I could run my fingers down his cheek. "Samantha Delany. It's got a great ring to it, don't you think?"

I could only nod until I had control of myself. So damn emotional. Ugh. I sucked in a deep breath and smiled at him. "Yeah, it does. Sam Delany." I laughed. "I knew you'd see things my way."

"Don't I usually?" he asked.

The nurse smiled at our conversation as she continued to tap keys and shift the wand. "The rest of the appointment is just taking measurements and stuff. I heard Dad mention an interview, so if you have to go, you won't be missing anything dramatic."

I blew a kiss at the phone. "Call me after the interview," I said.

"I will," Chase said. "I've been told I have a couple days between shows after Columbus, so I'm going to fly back. We'll do the nursery all in pink or whatever you want then, okay?"

I said goodbye, and we hung up. As the appointment wound down, I found myself alternating between a confusing welter of emotions. I was ecstatic at the thought of having a daughter, and I was so grateful to Chase for making the effort to be as involved as possible in the ultrasound; on the other hand, I was still terrified.

I stopped in the hallway as the thought hit me. I'd been skirting it for a while, but now it was out there. I was terrified. I'd never had to take care of anyone but myself. Even now that I was married to Chase, I was still basically independent most of the time. I'd held babies on a handful of occasions, when friends had them, but that was it. I had never interacted with a baby for longer than ten or fifteen minutes.

And Chase would be gone for much of it.

Could I do this?

I managed to make it home before the emotions overtook me. I sobbed in the bathroom for nearly an hour, only pulling myself out of it when my phone rang. I stared at the screen with the picture of Chase, trying to suck down the tears and rub away the redness. He'd still know I'd been crying, but there was nothing for it.

I sniffed, wiped my face, and slid the "answer" key across the screen. "Hi, baby."

"What's wrong, Jamie?" His voice was soft with concern.

"Nothing. Just hormones." I knew he wouldn't buy it, but I didn't want him to worry.

"Oh, come on, Jay. Don't feed me horseshit. What's up?"

I sighed. "Just…it's hard, sometimes."

"What is?"

"Having you gone." My voice was tiny, hesitant. "I know I signed up for it when I married you, and I love what you do. I'm so proud of you, but—it's just hard sometimes is all."

I heard Chase sigh, a deep, soulful sound. "I know, Jay. It's hard for me, too, you know that, right? I hate being away from you. I hate that I wasn't there with you in the office today. I hate that I'll probably miss other big stuff while I'm gone." His voice strengthened. "I can make you this promise, though: I will be there with you when Samantha is born. I don't care if I have to walk off stage in the middle of a show—I'll be there. You have my word."

I nodded, even though he couldn't see me. "Okay. Thank you." I heard people in the background calling his name. "You should go. I love you. Call again when you can."

"I will. Love you. 'Bye." And he was gone.

I put my hand over my belly, picturing a girl with curly black hair and brown eyes. "We can do this, can't we, Samantha?"

As if she'd heard me, I felt a flutter in my belly, and then a sharp poke. My hand clapped over my mouth, and I sobbed in a hiccuping laugh as I realized I'd just felt my first kick.

I was really, actually, factually having a baby. A real live human being was going to come out of my hoo-ha.

Oh, shit.

Chapter 3: Anna

I WATCHED CHASE AND JEFF standing awkwardly side by side, Miller Lites in hand, their faces locked in matching rictuses of agony. Jamie's mother-in-law shrieked particularly loudly when Jamie unwrapped the third set of onesies with cute little sayings like "Mommy's little monster" on them. Chase rubbed his forehead with the rim of his beer bottle at his mother's high-pitched squeals of excitement.

"Chase! Look!" Kelly Delany said, rushing over to her son. "This one says 'Daddy's Girl' on it! Isn't it just adorable!"

Chase stifled a sigh. "Yes, Mom, it's adorable. It's as adorable as the last fifty-seven I've seen. They're all adorable."

Kelly shot her son a scathing glare. "Well, don't sound so enthusiastic. I wouldn't want you to get overexcited or anything. It's not like you're about to be a father or anything."

Chase spoke into his beer bottle. "I'm excited to have a baby, Mom. What I'm not excited about is sitting around watching a bunch of women squawk about diapers and trade breastfeeding secrets."

Kelly huffed. "Then why are you here?"

Chase rolled the side of the bottle across his forehead. "I don't *know*, Mom. *Some*one told me I had to be here." He shot a dirty look at Jamie. "I've always sort of thought baby showers were a women-only thing. Guess I was wrong."

Jamie sighed. "Fine, leave, then. I just thought you would want to share in this experience." She gave him the dirty look right back. "Guess I was wrong."

"Fuck me," Chase muttered. "Don't turn this into something it's not. I'm excited for the *baby*, Jay. I couldn't care less about diapers and bizarre little shirts that snap together under her ass. I don't know."

Jay glared at him, then relented. "Fine. You're such a guy, Chase."

"Well, no shit," he muttered. "Was it the cock that gave it away, or the balls?"

I nearly snorted diet Coke out of my nose at that.

"It was the fact that you're a jackass, I'm pretty sure. Or the giant asshole where your face is supposed to be."

I did snort soda out my nose at that. "Jay, I'm sorry, but I don't think any guy on earth likes baby showers," I said.

Jay glared at me. "You're not helping, Anna."

"Actually, I like baby showers, and I have a cock," Lane—Jamie's GBFF (gay best friend forever)—said, raising his hand.

"Yeah," I said, "But you don't count. You're basically a girl."

Lane shrugged. "Yeah. But I'm still male. I'm on both sides with this one."

I glanced at Jeff. "You want to leave, too?"

He examined me carefully, then looked around the room and back to me. "You really have to ask?"

I sighed. "Ugh. Men." I looked at Jamie. "I think we have to let them leave for a while."

Jay waved her hand without looking up from her phone. "Fine. I already said fine."

Chase groaned. "But we all know what 'fine' means."

She clicked the button on the top of her phone to put it to sleep, and then gave Chase a sickly sweet smile. "Yeah, but we wouldn't our men to be bored, would we? Go get drunk or something. Just go."

Chase set his bottle down and grabbed Jeff by the shoulder, dragging him away and pushing him toward the door. "Let's go now, before they change their minds. God knows we don't want to get stuck playing fucking baby bingo or some shit."

I laughed at that, then fell silent when Jamie glared at me. Jeff mouthed I love you as Chase dragged him out the door. Jamie stared at the door, then turned back to the stack of wrapped gifts. "We're not playing baby bingo, are we, Jamie?" I asked, suddenly suspicious.

She huffed, looking offended. "No!" She lifted a box from the floor beside her. "Would I make you play something as dumb as that? We're playing 'pin the sperm on the egg.'"

I choked on my Coke a third time, spewing it out of my mouth and nose, coughing and laughing. "We're playing *what*?" Kelly patted me on the back and handed me a paper towel. I patted my yoga pants dry and wiped my face. "Are you serious?"

Jamie stood up slowly and made her way to a wall, where she had taped a filmy piece of plastic-y material. It was yellow with a cartoon diagram of the female reproductive organs in purple. Along one edge of the uterus was a pink dot with a bizarre smiley face on it. Jamie showed us little black squiggly bits with bulbous heads, fixed with a pin near the head, obviously meant to represent sperm.

I groaned. "You're serious." I took one of the sperms from Jamie and examined it, shaking my head. "Where did you find this, Jay? And we're not seriously going to play this, are we?"

Jamie snatched the sperm from my hand and set it neatly in a pile with the others on her coffee table. "I found it online. It looks like fun. There was actual baby bingo, but that's dumb."

"This isn't dumb?" I demanded.

She glared at me. "No, it's cute and funny." At my skeptical expression, she gave me a hurt look. "What the fuck do I know about baby showers, Anna? I've only even held a baby a handful of times in my life. I've never been to a baby shower before. I'm not the kind of girl you invite to baby showers. Bachelorette parties, yes. Baby showers, no. I'm trying, okay? I don't know how to do this. I don't know how to be—" She sobbed suddenly.

I levered myself out of the chair and wrapped her in a hug. "It's fine, Jay. It's great. We'll have lots of fun pinning little spermies to happy eggs."

"It's not about the fucking game, Anna!" Jamie pulled away from me to shoot me an evil look. "I don't know shit about babies or how to be a mother. And Chase is gone, and I don't know how to do this!"

I sighed, not wanting to admit my own very similar feelings. Kelly came up on Jamie's other side, joined by Lindsey, two of her friends, and several other girls I didn't know but thought were somehow connected to Chase's band.

"I'm scared, Anna." Jamie whispered it into my ear so the other women wouldn't hear.

Kelly turned Jamie's face with a palm. "You're allowed to be scared, Jamie. Every woman is scared for her first baby. I think you're scared for every baby, no matter how many you have. Babies are scary. No one here thinks any less of you for being afraid."

"What if something goes wrong and Chase isn't here?" Jamie said. "What if I go into labor early? What if we have this baby and I'm a shitty mom? What if I fuck her up? I don't want to fuck up my daughter, but I will. I fuck everything up."

I laughed, crying with her now. "No, you don't, Jay. You'll be a great mother. You're not going to fuck up your daughter. You won't, I promise you."

Jamie sniffled, then looked at me. "Are you scared, Anna?"

I laughed again. "Jay, I wake up in the middle of the night having panic attacks. Every night for the last month I've woken up at two in the morning, barely able to breathe, panicking. You guys can't tell Jeff because he'll just worry and I need him to be the one who's not worrying. I'm terrified, Jay." I knew I shouldn't say the next part, but I did anyway. "I wish I had my best friend. I know you live in New York now, but...I sometimes wish you didn't. I know you're happy here with Chase and everything, and it's selfish of me, but I just wish sometimes that we could have our babies together."

Jamie lost it again. "I'm not happy, Anna! That's the worst part! Chase is on tour. He's gone more than he's here. I talk to him several times a day, and I'm so thankful for that. He's making a huge effort to keep in contact with me and I realize that, and I appreciate it. He FaceTimed me instead of doing an interview with a magazine just so he could sort of be there when we found out Samantha's gender. It was so sweet. But…I'm still alone when I go to bed and when I wake up. When he's here, I'm deliriously happy. But…he's only here until Wednesday, and then he's gone again right up until I'm full-term."

Kelly subtly shooed the other girls away so it was just her, Jamie, and me. "I might have an idea, Jay. I'm not sure it will work, but…you could always stay with me. The last trimester is always the hardest, and you really shouldn't be alone. I can help you, and then when you go into labor, Chase can just fly in to Detroit instead of New York. I know you and I don't know each other all that great, but I'd love to have the opportunity to fix that." She picked at her cuticles with a fingernail while she spoke, as if afraid of rejection.

Jamie's eyes lit up with relief. "Really? That would be so cool! I just…I don't want to do this alone. And that way Anna and I could have our babies together."

I pulled Jamie and Kelly into a hug. "I think it's perfect."

Jamie sniffled. "Thanks, Kelly. You're the best."

Kelly just smiled and hugged us together.

We played Pin the Sperm on the Egg, which was actually really fun. It degenerated into a frenzy of sex jokes and all-around bawdy silliness, and by the time the shower was over, Jamie seemed to be in better spirits. The boys came back about an hour after the party was over, and they were surprisingly sober. I never thought I'd see the day, but they seemed comfortable with each other.

It was still awkward for me, sometimes, seeing both Jeff and Chase together, but as time passed and the memories faded, so did the awkwardness. Jeff and Chase were laughing at a joke as they clomped through the foyer of Jamie and Chase's beyond-fabulous Manhattan brownstone. Jamie and I exchanged a pleased glance at the way our men seemed to have bonded while they were gone. I gave Jamie an *I told you so* smirk, and she just rolled her eyes in acknowledgment.

When the party mess was cleaned up, Jeff, Chase, Kelly, Jamie, and I all sat down in the living room.

"So, Chase." Kelly sat on the arm of the couch next to her son. "I was talking to Jamie while you and Jeff were gone. I was thinking it may be a good idea for her come stay with me in Birmingham for her last trimester. She really needs someone to help her while you're gone."

Chase looked from his wife to his mother, and then stood up with a sigh. He crossed the room to look out the window onto the busy street beyond. "Meaning she'd have the baby in Detroit, rather than here."

"I know it's not what we originally planned," Jamie said, moving to stand next to Chase. "But...I think it would be good for me."

Chase didn't answer for a long time. "It's that hard for you here by yourself, huh?" He ran his palm back and forth over his head, a gesture I knew meant he was upset.

"Yeah, it really is." She moved to stand in front of him, wrapping her arms around his waist and staring up at him. "I like your mom a lot. It would be nice to get to know her, for one thing. And for another, I'm barely twenty weeks along, and it's already getting harder for me to move around. When I'm thirty-four weeks and can't get up without a fricking crane, being here alone while you're touring would be...god, it'd be impossible."

Chase nodded. "I get it." He let out a long breath. "So you're moving back to Detroit. Okay, then."

Jamie frowned up at him. "No, Chase. I'm not *moving* anywhere. I'm staying with Kelly temporarily until I have the baby. By then your tour will be over, and we'll come back home together." She put her hand to the back of Chase's head, tilting his face down to hers. "This is home. Here, with you. I know this tour is important, and I'd never ever ask you to stop, or change it, or cut it short. I just—I need help, baby."

The hard, tense set of Chase's shoulders relaxed. "You're right. You're right. It is a good idea. I just—I wish I could be here. I wish it wasn't necessary. That's all." He lowered his face to hers for a kiss.

When their lips met, I looked away and found Jeff watching me. He tilted his head toward the door, indicating that it was time to go. Kelly had already sneaked out the front door, and when I turned to say goodbye to Jamie, I realized why: She and Chase were lip-locked in a kiss that had all the signs of not stopping, regardless of who was or wasn't in the room. I felt myself blush when Chase's hands slid up the backs of Jamie's thighs to pull her against him.

"On that note, I think it's time to go," I said.

Jamie lifted up on her toes and peeked at me over Chase's shoulder. "'Bye, Anna. 'Bye, Jeff. Call me tomorrow."

"Sure thing. I think we're leaving after lunch, so we can do breakfast together."

Jamie just waved at me with one hand, already lost in Chase's mouth. I turned away before awkwardness descended any more thickly on me. When we were in a cab headed toward our hotel, Jeff twisted on the seat to look at me. "You all right?"

I shrugged. "Yeah, why wouldn't I be?" Jeff just frowned, but I knew what he was getting at. He wouldn't be able to say it out loud, but I knew. I decided to put him out of his misery. "I'm fine, Jeff. I'm happy for Jamie and Chase. Did you have fun with him?"

Jeff nodded. "Yeah, once I got past that it was fucking pretty-boy Chase I was hanging with, yeah." That was as close as Jeff would come to acknowledging the elephant in the room that was my previous relationship with Chase. "He's cool. We drank some scotch at the sports bar down the street and watched the UConn-Nebraska game. I'm not really into the whole March Madness thing, but I'll watch a game here and there. Chase is the same way."

"I have no idea what March Madness is," I said.

"College basketball playoffs, basically." He glanced at me to gauge the effect of his next words. "Chase is pretty mixed up about the whole being gone while Jamie's pregnant business. He admitted that he's thought about cutting the tour short to be with her full-time."

"He really can't do that," I said. "This tour is a make-it-or-break-it thing. They're getting big, but this tour can really cement them as one of the biggest up-and-coming bands in the business. If they cut the tour short, it could ruin all the progress they've made. They're not so big that they can do whatever they want, not yet at least."

Jeff nodded. "He said the same thing, basically. I think Jamie going back to the D until the baby's out is a good plan."

"I think so, too. And I'm really excited that she'll be around for a while. It would be so cool if we could have our babies at the same time." I smirked at Jeff. "You know what else is a really good idea? Finding out the gender on Monday."

Jeff let his head fall back onto the seat with a sigh. "Here we go again."

I just laughed.

Jeff squeezed my hand gently as the ultrasound technician prepped me, lining my belly with white towels and splooging a glop of frigid blue goo onto my stomach. The lights were dim, a computer monitor on the wall opposite the chair showing a black screen with indecipherable words and abbreviations on either side. My name, Anna Cartwright, was written across the top of the screen. I was still getting used to writing "Cartwright" as my last name, but I felt a thrill every time I did.

"So," the technician said, rubbing the tip of the wand into the goo on my belly, "you're not finding out the gender?"

"That's what *he* says." I jerked my thumb at Jeff. "I want to know, but he doesn't. Maybe you can tell me and he can cover his ears or something."

"That's cheating," Jeff said with a grin."

"Well, we could do it that way," the technician said. "I wouldn't recommend it, though. You should know or not know together, as a couple. I will say, though, that you'd be surprised by how many couples have this same argument in here. It's not uncommon."

"I just want to be able to decorate the nursery." I watched the screen shifting as she slid the wand around my belly.

"Okay," the nurse said. "Look here, you can see the head and a little arm, see it?"

Jeff and I looked at each other, then the screen. I clenched Jeff's hand as we saw our baby for the first time. My heart stuttered, leapt, and then began hammering as the reality of our baby hit me.

"Can you tell what it is?" Jeff asked.

"I"m looking," the nurse said. "I want to get a fix on the heartbeat first, though. Here, listen."

She tapped a key on the keyboard, and then another, and the sound of the heartbeat filled the room. I covered my mouth with my free hand, hearing a real live heart beating inside me. I looked at Jeff, who was as transfixed as I was.

There was something odd about the heartbeat, an odd overlapping in the rhythm. It made my stomach drop. "Is that how a heartbeat is supposed to sound?" I asked.

"I'm looking into that, just wait a second," the nurse said. "I think—" But she cut herself off as she wiggled the wand around, sliding it from one spot to another, the sound of the heartbeat distorting.

"What is it? Is everything okay?" Jeff demanded.

"She's fine, it's just...wait...now listen." She swiveled the wand a fraction, and the distortion of the heartbeat cleared, and then she swiveled it in the opposite direction, making the sound fade, distort, and then clear up again. "Hear that?" She turned in her seat to grin at me.

I felt an inkling of realization strike me. "Is that...*two* heartbeats?"

"Two? Like twins?" Jeff asked.

I turned to look at him, seeing surprise on his face as I'm sure it was on mine. The nurse repeated the effect of producing two distinct heartbeats, then tapped a few more keys and searched my belly some more. I watched the view on the monitor shift and adjust, and then, as she brought the wand around to my side, I saw it, saw *them*, two distinct forms. Four arms, four legs. Two heads. Two heartbeats.

Two babies. *Holy shit.*

The nurse searched and tapped some more, and then pointed at the screen once more. "Congratulations, Mr. and Mrs. Cartwright. You're having twins!"

Jeff and I traded stunned glances. Jeff's mouth flapped open and closed as he tried to speak. "Twins? How—how—*twins?*"

The nurse just laughed as she continued to adjust the wand for different views. "That's a very common reaction, actually. Are there any twins on either side of your families?"

I nodded my head, almost absently. "Yeah, yeah, we both have twins in our family."

"Well, there you go. It's a genetic thing, although there are rare cases of twins in families with no history of it." She printed out some pictures of the babies—*babies, plural...oh, god*—and put them in an envelope, then proceeded to swivel the wand and tap on the keyboard, sometimes making parts of the screen turn technicolor. "So, do you still want it to be a surprise, now that you know you're having twins?"

Jeff and I exchanged glances.

I touched his cheek so he looked at me. "Jeff? You're the one who wanted it to be a surprise in the first place."

He shook his head slowly. "I think...I think we've got enough of a surprise now."

"So you want to know?" The nurse adjusted the wand to focus on one of the babies. "Well... it looks like this one is...ooh, this is a great potty shot. It's a girl. See?" She moved the wand, searching for the best view once more, talking to herself. "Okay. Baby number two...where are you? There you are. That's your head, and there's your legs, come on, baby, give a good look. Ah, gotcha. Baby number two is...a boy! They're fraternal twins, a boy and a girl."

I sucked in a deep breath to calm myself. "God, twins." I looked at Jeff, who seemed to be still struggling with shock. "You called it, remember?"

He shook his head, then met my eyes. "I called it? Oh, yeah. Way back, just after I proposed." He laughed. "I did, didn't I?"

"We're having twins, Jeff." I said it out loud again.

"Oh, god. Oh, god. Twins." He gave me an odd smile. "So, Miss Interior Decorator. How are we doing the nursery now that we're having a boy *and* a girl?"

I just shook my head. "I have no idea. I like green?"

Jeff laughed. "What I said in the first place? Nice, Anna." He turned to the nurse. "So aside from the fact that there's two babies in there, does everything else look good?"

She nodded. "Yes, everything looks great. All the measurements are right on target for twins. The high-risk doctor will want to talk to you, though."

Jeff's face paled. "The high-risk doctor? Why? I thought you said things were good?"

She patted his hand. "Any time a woman carries twins, she's considered high-risk. Giving birth is complicated enough with one baby, so when you have two, we just have to be extra careful so the mother and the children are all safe and healthy. It's just a precaution, Mr. Cartwright. No need to worry."

When we were back home, I kicked off my shoes and lowered myself to the couch. Jeff sat next to me and lifted my feet onto his lap, rubbing my instep with his thumbs. Several minutes passed in silences, until I felt myself drowsing.

As I was about to drift off, I felt Jeff's hand cover my belly. I felt his face touch my stomach, and opened my eyes sleepily. His eyes were locked on mine, molten brown love, tender hands caressing my belly. "Caleb and Niall," he whispered. "Caleb *and* Niall."

I smiled at him, brushing his hair across his forehead. "Caleb and Niall. A son and a daughter. Are you ready for this?"

He laughed. "No. Not even close. But it's happening. It's real." He leaned toward me, taking my lips with his. "And I'm glad."

"You are? You're glad?" I spoke into his lips as they covered mine, tasted mine.

"Mmm-hmmm. Of course." His fingers touched my cheek, then traced down the curve of my neck. "A little nervous, I admit. But glad. I'm excited to be a daddy."

"I'm excited to be a mommy." I twisted and lay back on the couch, pulling Jeff over me. "I'm also excited for you to get me naked and plunder me on the couch."

Jeff pushed my shirt up over my head, and I unclasped my bra while he tugged my pants off. A few more moments passed, and I was naked and wrapping my knees over his shoulders and burying my fingers in his hair while his tongue dipped into me, slowly at first, in circles and gliding upward strokes. I let him tongue me into a frenzy, but when I was on the cusp of orgasm, I pulled him away, pulled him up to me. He'd shed his shirt and unbuttoned his jeans at some point. I slid my fingers under the band of his boxers and freed his heavy erection, pushing his jeans away and guiding him to me. He nudged my knee aside so my foot planted flat on the floor, the other stretched out along the back of the couch. Kneeling above me, Jeff put one foot next to mine on the floor and nestled his tip into my folds, one hand on the armrest of the couch just past my head, the other caressing my face and my breasts and my belly, then dipping down to cup my mound. I lifted my hips and he slid in, both of us sighing as he filled me. His fingers slipped between the joining of our bodies and circled my clit, driving gasps from me.

He was only barely moving, but something about the angle and the placement of our bodies on the couch gave him incredible leverage, letting each stroke drive deep and slick along all the best nerve endings. I needed more. God, more. I pushed up off the floor with one foot, bracing the other on the opposite end of the couch, lifting my hips to crash against his in a pleasingly punishing rhythm. Jeff seemed surprised by my sudden desperation. I wasn't sure where it was coming from, but as he slid into me, driving deeper with each thrust, I found myself needing more, more, even though I'd had him just the night before. Each stroke of his shaft into me drove me crazier, wilder, incited my need.

"God, Jeff. I love you so much. Don't stop, please." I clutched his ass with desperate fingers, pulling him into me, thrusting up to meet him stroke for stroke until we were thrashing on the couch together, frantic, moaning into mouths and against shoulders, riding the cusp of climax together. Then his fingers found my clit and his mouth found my nipple, and I passed over the edge, screaming his name. I clamped down with inner muscles and arched my entire body off the couch, crushing my soft folds into his hardness and pulsating in shallow thrusts, whimpering and gasping as he hit me deep inside. I felt his stomach tense, heard his breath catch and felt his rhythm falter.

"Give it to me, Jeff. Give it all to me, right now." I wrapped my arms around his neck and pulled him down against me, relishing his weight on me, the feel of his hips hard against mine, his shaft piercing deep and his balls slapping against me, his fingers in my hair and on my nipple.

"You want it, baby?" He kissed me, quick and sloppy, pumping into me madly now.

"God, yes, Jeff. Let me feel you fill me up. Come for me, love. Come hard." I dragged my fingers down his back and felt him shudder, felt him tense. I kissed his temple, his cheek, his shoulder, his chin, whispered his name into his mouth and wrapped my legs around his hips as he came, and I kissed his quivering mouth as he gasped my name with his release.

After the shocks had faded, I curled into the back of the couch, holding Jeff close as we both shuddered. "I think that was the best couch sex we've ever had," I said.

He made a growl of agreement in his chest. "Yeah. Although, once we have the twins, our days of rocking couch sex are numbered."

I laughed. "I think once we have the twins, our days of sex of any kind are numbered."

He lifted up to look at me in mock horror. "Don't *say* that!"

I quirked an eyebrow at him. "You know we can't have sex for six weeks after I give birth, right?"

He put his face into my shoulder and pretended to sob. "More weeks without sex? I'll die. I'll die dead of blue balls."

"No, you won't," I said, cradling his head with my hands. "I'll take care of you—don't worry."

"Promise?" He looked comically serious. I think he may have been serious.

I laughed and kissed him. "Yes, baby. I promise. No blue balls for you."

I found myself wondering about my own need for orgasms, though. I know you weren't supposed to put anything in your vagina for six weeks after birth, but I could I let Jeff twiddle my button? Or would I be so stretched out that he wouldn't be able to find it? I kept these worries to myself. Jeff seemed horrified enough as it was.

Twins. Holy shit.

Chapter 4: Jamie

I RUBBED MY SHOULDER beneath the bra strap, trying to alleviate the twinge in the muscle. Kelly frowned at me, watching me massage my shoulder.

"Something wrong with your shoulder?" she asked, stuffing the last of my maternity clothes into a suitcase.

I shrugged, rolling my shoulder. "No, I'm fine. My shoulder's just been achy recently. No big deal." I zipped my toiletries case closed and tossed it into the suitcase next to my hair straightener and blow dryer. "That should be it. Let's go."

Kelly didn't move, just stared at me thoughtfully. "Have you had any other odd feelings? Achy back, nausea as if morning sickness was coming back? Anything like that?"

I zipped the suitcase closed, set it on the floor, and pulled the handle up with a *click*. "I've been a little nauseous, yeah, but I think it's just heartburn."

Kelly shook her head, chin-length black hair bouncing. "Don't ignore that stuff. We're going to the doctor as soon as we get to Detroit. How long have you been having those symptoms?" Kelly was a nurse, I had found out, and was taking her role as my caretaker very seriously.

"Symptoms? Why are you calling them symptoms? It's just normal pregnancy stuff, right?" I buttoned up my sweater, stuffed my phone and charger in my purse, and gave my beautiful home one last look-over.

It was clean, tidied, and dark. Mrs. Lettis was coming over once a week to check on things for us, which she would have done for free, I'm pretty sure, but Chase insisted on paying her. I locked the front door behind me, and let Kelly take the suitcase and stuff it into the trunk of the waiting cab.

"Because they very well could be symptoms," Kelly said.

I slid into the seat, puffing embarrassingly from the exertion necessary to just sit down in a car. I was twenty-three weeks now, and officially the size and shape of a beluga. I wasn't sure I'd be able to get out of bed by the time I was full-term, if I kept getting bigger. Stupid Anna, even with her twins, still wasn't as big as me. I didn't get it.

"Symptoms of what?"

"Preeclampsia." Something in her tone of voice had me worried.

"I've heard that word, but I don't know what it is," I said.

Kelly patted my knee. "It's complicated. I'm not going to worry you until we know for sure. Just be sure to tell me if you have any more things like that. Even if you're positive it's just usual pregnancy discomfort, tell me. Okay?"

I was worried now, but no sense in telling her that. I just shrugged. "Okay."

We chatted aimlessly the rest of the cab ride to the train station. Once we were in our seats, Kelly pulled out a paperback and was soon lost to the world. I dug my iPad out of my purse and opened the browser. I typed "preeclampsia" into the Google search bar and brought up the first hit, a .org website dedicated solely to preeclampsia. The more I read, the more frightened I became. By the time I'd read everything on the website, I was in full-blown panic attack mode.

"Kelly." I closed the cover to my iPad and met Kelly's eyes over the top of her book, a bodice-ripper, by the looks of it. "You think I have preeclampsia?"

Kelly sighed and set the book face down on her thigh. Her kind brown eyes, so much like Chase's, searched mine and were soft with worry. "You

Googled it, didn't you?" I nodded. "Jamie, it's going to be okay. I don't know that you do. I just don't want to ignore the possibility."

"But I'm experiencing everything listed on the website. Everything. And it said there's no cure but to induce labor or to abort. I'm not—I can't—I mean—"

Kelly leaned forward and took my hands in hers. "You're freaking yourself out needlessly. You're fine. Samantha is fine. Okay? We'll go see Dr. Rayburn first thing, I promise."

I took several deep breaths and tried to push away my panic, my tears, my sense of impending doom—which, by the way, was also one of the possible symptoms. For something which had no cure except to have the baby, and I wasn't even close to full-term yet.

I managed to calm myself down enough that I didn't hyperventilate, but it was close. I marinated in my own worry for most of the excruciatingly long train ride from New York to Detroit. When Chase called, he picked up on my worry within minutes, but I wasn't ready to saddle him with the possibilities yet, especially since, as Kelly said, I wasn't even sure I had preeclampsia. It was hard not to tell Chase, though. He was, beneath everything else, my best friend. I told him everything. So to keep this from him, even if it was just a worry at that point, was painful. I wanted him to comfort me, to tell me it was fine, that I was just being silly. But if I told him, he'd worry. And when he worried, he would be off his game, and this tour *had* to go well.

By the time we pulled into Detroit some fifteen hours later, I was delirious from exhaustion. I'd run through every possibility in my head a dozen times, from an emergency C-section as soon as I saw the doctor to being hospitalized for the next twelve weeks to being told I was an idiot for worrying so much over nothing. Kelly had slept most of the way, and I'd read the book she'd brought, as well as another one I had on my iPad. I'd watched half of the first season of *Downton Abbey*. I was bored, scared, tired, cramped, worried, and panicked. And horny. How could I be horny at a time like this? I had no answer for myself, and no relief in sight until I saw Chase again in a couple weeks.

Kelly woke up as we pulled into the station, took one look at me, and groaned. "You've been working yourself into a fit the entire time, haven't you?"

I just shrugged and tugged my sweater higher up my shoulders. I knew if I answered her out loud, I'd snap, and she didn't deserve that. We made our way to Kelly's car in the long-term parking lot and shoved my suitcase in the backseat of her Lincoln MKZ. Chase had wanted to buy her something fancier, but she'd refused to let him, he claimed.

So he'd gotten her the Lincoln and had it stuffed with every available option. He'd laughed when he related how she'd chewed his ear off after the car was delivered. I don't know what she was complaining about; it was a nice car that I wouldn't mind driving, if it had been practical to even own a car in New York City.

I fell asleep in the car and didn't wake up until Kelly gently shook my shoulder an hour later, sitting in her driveway. It was past two in the morning, and I followed Kelly sleepily as she unlocked her front door and showed my my room. I didn't even look around me at Kelly's house. I fell facefirst into the bed, felt Kelly slip my shoes off, tug the blankets free from beneath me, and drape them over me. I couldn't even summon the strength to murmur a thanks to her. And yet, even in the grip of utter exhaustion, I dreamed of being chained to a hospital bed for the next three months.

I woke up in a sweat, near tears, and rubbed my wrists where I'd felt the shackles in my dream. As I fell asleep, I felt the dream coming back, felt the panic, the bone-deep fear.

The next morning—or, well, it was past noon by the time I woke up—Kelly forced a healthy breakfast down my throat and shooed me into her car. My OB/GYN in New York had referred me to a colleague of hers in Detroit, and had insisted I go in for an appointment when I arrived. Now that

Kelly had so kindly instilled in me the fear of pre-eclampsia, I was all too willing to get poked and prodded again, if it meant putting my mind at ease.

Two hours and half a dozen tests later, I sat in the passenger seat of Kelly's car, sobbing hysterically into the phone while Chase begged me to calm down and tell him what the problem was. Eventually, Kelly took the phone from me and explained preeclampsia and all its attendant issues and worries to him. By the time she'd educated Chase on my problem, I had calmed down enough to carry on an intelligible conversation.

Kelly handed the phone back to me and I pressed it to my ear, sniffling but calm. "Hi, baby," I said. "So. How's the tour?" I asked, with overly fake enthusiasm.

"Fuck the tour," Chase growled. "I'm coming back."

"No, baby," I said. "Not yet. You're almost done at this point. Just finish the tour. You can't quit now, Chase, and you know it. Doctor Rayburn said we just have to watch my blood pressure for now. Worst-case scenario, they'll induce me at thirty-two weeks. I'll call you every day and tell how I'm doing, okay?"

Chase growled again. "No, it's not okay. I should be there with you. I should be the one taking care of you."

"You will be. You have to finish the tour, Chase. You *have* to. The label will be pissed if you quit."

"I'm gonna worry more than ever now."

I sighed. "I know. I didn't want to tell you, but...I'm scared. I know it's going to be okay, but I'm scared."

"Goddamn it, Jay." I heard the anguish in his voice. "I should *be* there."

"You're where you have to be for now. If something comes up, I'll be the first one to call you, okay? I promise."

"But if something comes up, I'll be hours away. What if—what if I don't get there in time?"

Kelly took the phone from me. "Listen, son. I'm here with her. This is why she came to Detroit. I'm a nurse. I know what to look for. I'll monitor her blood pressure and make sure she rests. I'll take care of her. You need to focus on doing your job. Keep your fans happy."

"Okay, Mom," I heard him say. "Just...take care of her, okay?"

"I will, Chase. It'll be fine."

I took the phone back, told Chase I loved him, and hung up. Kelly tried making conversation on the way back to her house, but I ignored her. I didn't mean to be rude, but I just couldn't summon the will to care. Eventually, she relented with a sigh and turned on the radio to a pop station. Even Rihanna couldn't get me out of my funk, it seemed.

Bed rest sucked. I wouldn't let Kelly take time off work until absolutely necessary, especially since

Beaumont Hospital, where she worked, was barely a ten-minute drive from her house. Which meant, of course, that I was home alone and relegated to complete bed rest. Like, don't get up to pee unless you absolutely have to. I've always been an active person. I wasn't a gym rat by any stretch of the imagination, but I liked to do stuff. I worked hard, I played hard, and I kept busy. I've never been the type to sit around and watch TV all day, and now, suddenly, that and read was all I had to do. For the first couple days, I watched every movie Kelly owned, which was quite a few. She had everything from *The Breakfast Club* to *Walk the Line*, even a few action/adventure movies featuring hot shirtless men. After I'd gone through her movie collection, I started in on daytime television programming.

Fuck daytime programming.

I watched all her movies again, and then went through all the movies available on her premium cable package's On Demand section, even the ones I'd never heard of and didn't really like. I even watched *3000 Miles to Graceland* twice.

At which point, a single week had passed.

Fuck bedrest.

Fuck preeclampsia.

When Kelly came back from work at the end of the second week, I begged her to help me find something to pass the time. She stifled her laughter and brought out her knitting kit.

I just stared at her.

"You expect me to knit? Do you know me at *all*?" I held the needles in each hand like knives, pretending to stab her. "What am I going to knit? Socks? Sweaters?"

Kelly laughed and fended me off with a clipboard. "Figuring that out will be part of what passes the time." She gestured at the TV. "You know I've got Netflix on there, right?"

I frowned at her. "What?"

"The TV. When I went to finally buy a new TV after having the same one since nineteen-ninety, the salesman talked me into getting this fancy one here. It's a smart TV, apparently. You can surf the Web on it, which I'm not entirely sure what the point of that is, but you can." She picked up the remote and hit a button, bringing up a menu bar across the bottom of the screen. "I had to have the Best Buy Geek Squad come out and set all this up for me, but now that I have it and know how to work it, it's awesome. Netflix has pretty much everything, including entire seasons of shows—"

I rolled my eyes and snatched the remote from her. "I know what it is, Kelly. Why the hell didn't you tell me about this two weeks ago? I was about to start watching all your movies through for the third time. Jesus."

Kelly flushed with embarrassment. "Sorry, I just...I forgot. I guess I just thought you'd be able to figure it out on your own or something. Technology is my worst enemy." She sat on the couch next to me and untied her white Keds. "When the hospital started the transition to tablet computers, I seriously almost lost my job because I couldn't figure them out. When Chase insisted I have a smart phone, I had to take it in to the Verizon store and have them show me how to use the damn thing. I couldn't even figure out how to answer a stupid phone call. I kept hanging up on Chase and then redialing him."

I laughed with her as I flipped through the Netflix options. Thank sweet baby Jesus for Netflix. I might actually come out of this whole bed-rest thing with most of my sanity intact.

I wondered if bed rest meant I couldn't have sex with Chase. That would be bad, very, very bad. The doctor hadn't said specifically no sex, but she'd said I can't do anything to raise my blood pressure. Chase definitely had a tendency to raise my blood pressure, you might say.

The next day while Kelly was working, I sat down with the second season of *The Walking Dead* queued up and a reusable Whole Foods bag full of colored string. Okay, *fine*, they were skeins of yarn, I suppose. I chose yellow, orange, green, and red yarn, pulled up a "how to knit" video on YouTube, and got started.

It took three days of clicking needles and unthreading my knots before I got the hang of it and was able to start trying to make something for real. I'd finished *The Walking Dead* and was going through *Spartacus*. The first thing I knitted was an unrecognizable, misshapen thing that vaguely resembled something a Rasta might wear over his dreads, if knitted by a blind and drunk old woman. I had meant it to be…well, I didn't really have any idea what it was supposed to be. A hat, maybe. Or a pillowcase. It could function as either, really.

By the time I was done with the pillowcase/hat, I had watched through a couple seasons of *Sex and the City*. I'd already seen the entire series—and all the movies—but it was a comfort-food kind of thing. I could quote my favorite lines from the first season to the last, and to rewatch it—for the third or fourth time, possibly—was like hanging out with old friends. I could partially tune it out and try to focus on actually knitting—or crocheting or whatever—something useful.

I managed a scarf, first. It was about four feet long and six inches wide and had holes big enough you could fit your fist through them, but it was recognizably a scarf.

#Winning.

Kelly laughed her ass off at my scarf, and then showed me how to tighten my knots or whatever the hell they're called. Stitches? Loops? They're knots, fancy knots. So I made another scarf, this one longer and wider and with fewer gaping holes. It was pink and purple, so I gave it to Kelly, who actually wore it, bless her heart. I think she did it to be nice to me, since it was warm out and the scarf was the ugliest thing I'd ever seen. The edges curled and refused to lie flat, the ends were crooked, and the whole thing was just fucking ugly. But Kelly wore the thing to and from work for a solid week before I told her she didn't have to actually wear it. She looked relieved.

Now that I had more of a hang of it, I decided to make a pair of socks for Chase. Which was stupid, because they'd be more like something Santa Claus would wear over his boots or something, but still. I'd knit the damn things and give them to him, and he'd be grateful, damn it.

I managed one "sock" while I watched the best of John Cusack's eighties movies. By which I mean *Say Anything*, *Sixteen Candles*, and *Stand by Me*. I also tossed *High Fidelity* in there even though it's not technically an '80s movie, but it's awesome and has Jack Black in it.

Chase walked in at the end of *HiFi*, and I shrieked happily. I also might've peed a little.

No one told me about that, and I wish they had. I mean, I've heard all sorts of stand-up skits by women who have kids, but I thought it was a joke. Like, ha-ha, you pee by accident. So funny.

NO. Not funny. You really do pee by accident. I laughed too hard once watching *Liar, Liar*, and I peed so bad I had to change my panties. For real. I was so embarrassed I started a load of laundry, even though I was alone in the house and not supposed to lift baskets of clothes. So yeah. Pee. I thought about wearing a pad all the time.

Chase knelt beside me as I struggled to a sitting position on the couch. "I had a couple days between shows and decided to fly back and see you." He put a palm on my belly and the other on my cheek, kissing me slowly and deeply. My toes curled.

I pulled away, all too soon. "Don't get me worked up," I whispered. "I can't have sex."

Chase frowned. "What?"

"Yeah. Apparently orgasms raise your blood pressure or something, and that's a no-no." I slid my fingers through his hair, which was now long enough to be spiked in two-inch-tall gel-stiff prickles.

"That sucks, baby." He moved to sit next to me. "Here I was hoping to make you scream for me."

I moaned and thumped my forehead onto his shoulder. "I'm so mad. I miss you so much. I'm horny, and after I have the baby it'll be another six weeks before you can put anything into me."

Chase gripped my T-shirt in his fists, growling. "God. We're both gonna fucking die before we can make love again."

I grinned, putting my palms flat on his chest and pushing him backward until he was lying against the arm of the couch. "Just because I can't come," I said, unbuttoning his tight blue jeans, "doesn't mean you can't."

Chase sucked in a breath and caught my wrists. "But what about you?"

Ignoring his question, I freed my hands from his grip and unzipped him. "Commando?" I tugged his jeans down under his taut buttocks.

He groaned and watched me fist his erection with slow strokes. "I was planning on ravaging you into exhaustion. I thought it might take some of the stress away."

"It would have," I said, loving the blissful expression on his face as I worked his shaft with both hands, "and you're so sweet for thinking of me."

Chase lifted his head to quirk an eyebrow at me. "You're mocking me, aren't you?"

"You're a sad, strange little man," I said.

Chase laughed and let his head thump back again as I wrapped my palm around his thick mushroom head and twisted gently with a slight pumping motion, rolling my palm over his head and then twisting again. I thumbed the clear pearl of pre-come around his tip until he was slick under my hand, and then resumed the twisting, pumping motion, increasing in tempo until he was arching his back off the couch. I curled my other hand around his base and pumped him swiftly. The motions of each hand were hard to keep separate, but I made a challenge of it, twist and roll and pump. Chase groaned deep in his chest, and I felt him tense. I stopped all motion, just holding his cock in my fist and letting him back away from the edge.

Chase slammed his head against the arm of the couch. "Damn it, Jay. God, I was right there."

I slid off the couch to kneel on a pillow on the hardwood floor next to him. I leaned over him and ran my tongue up his throbbing length, then took him into my mouth and sucked once, twice, three times, just enough to get him moving, and then spitting him out and kissing back down his length. He tangled his fingers in my hair, holding the wayward strands away from my mouth, brushing my cheeks and my forehead, cupping my face, each touch tender. I planted kisses all the way down his shaft, then opened my mouth to take his sack between my lips, careful to cover my teeth. He hissed and cursed under his breath as I massaged his tender skin with my lips and tongue, holding his rigid cock in both hands.

When I thought he'd backed far enough away from the edge of climax, I resumed moving my hands up and down his length, tugging upward and sliding down to plunge my fingers against his base. He lifted his hips to meet each downward thrust of my hands, and now I lowered my mouth to him, taking his tip between my lips at each thrust.

The upward crush of hips grew desperate and his breathing ragged. "God, Jay. So fucking good. Feels...so good."

"Fuck my mouth, Chase." I whispered the words and then took him deep into my mouth.

He sucked in a raspy breath and let himself go, thrusting hard into me. I gripped his length with one hand, wrapping my lips around his tip and sucking hard as he thrust. When he pumped toward my throat, I sucked hard, and when he pulled away, I released the suction; when he thrust, I pumped his length. I cupped his balls in my other hand and massaged them, letting my middle finger extend back toward his taint and rubbing gently.

He buried both hands in my hair and held tight, not pushing me down, just holding, fisting his fingers in my curls. "God...*damn*. Oh, god, I'm close. So close. Don't tease me, baby. Let me come, please." I slowed my rhythm on him, just to tease him. "No, fuck no..." He wanted to pull me onto him, but didn't.

I laughed with my mouth still latched around his soft salty skin, and the buzz of my voice drove him wild. I let him thrust deep, relaxed my throat and took him deeper, clenching him with my fist and lips and my throat muscles, working him into a frenzy. His hips lifted off the couch, and he fluttered his cock in shallow, desperate thrusts. I didn't relent then but worked him faster, fingering his taint and fisting his base with a blurring hand, my grip loose so I was barely brushing his skin.

I felt him tense in my hands, heard him groan, curse, and gasp. He fell down onto the couch, then thrust again, and this time he did pull me against him, just a little, just enough to let me know he was about to explode. I hummed in my throat as I swallowed his tip as deep as I could, fisting him furiously.

"Oh, god…" Chase's fingers tightened in my hair. "I'm coming…"

He detonated with a groan. I felt his balls tense, and then hot liquid splashed down my throat. I backed away and took him deep again, setting a bobbing rhythm as he came again, and then again, spurting hard each time, groaning and cursing nonstop.

The payoff for him was almost as much of one for me. I loved watching him lose control, completely sated, eyes rolled back in blissed-out ecstasy. I continued to suck and stroke him as he softened, milking every last drop of pleasure from him.

Eventually I released him and sat next to him on the couch.

"Fuck, Jay," he said, pulling his jeans back on. "I think that may have been the best blow job you've ever given me."

I pushed his hands away and fastened his pants for him, enjoying the fact that he was panting, out of breath and sweating. "Good," I said. "That's the goal. Each BJ should be the best one yet."

"I think you succeeded, if that's your goal." He leaned in and kissed me, as he always did after I went down on him. "So how can I make you feel good?"

"You just did," I told him, sliding into the nook of his shoulder.

He snorted. "No, sweetheart. That was you making *me* feel good. You're getting things backward."

I laughed. "I get pleasure from that. Not sexual pleasure, like, it doesn't give me an 'O,' but I enjoy your reactions, making you feel good. We've talked about this."

"I know," he said, stroking my arm with his thumb. "But I still don't entirely believe you when you say you like it."

"Do you like going down on me?" I asked him.

"Yeah, for the same reasons you said. I like giving you pleasure, making you feel good."

"Well, there you go."

"So can I do that to you, then?" he asked.

I shook my head. "Sadly, no. There's nothing I'd love more than to have you munch my rug until I can't breathe, believe me. But at this point, it's not penetration that's the problem. It's my blood pressure. It's why I'm not supposed to exert myself. I have to stay off my feet so the effort of walking doesn't become too much. In which case, I'm pretty sure your expert skills in cunnilingus would make my blood pressure spike through the fucking roof."

Chase laughed. "Expert cunnilingus skills, huh?"

I nodded, patting his chest. "Yep. Masterful. You're an artisan of pussy-licking. A connoisseur of oral orgasm administration."

Chase laughed so hard my head bounced on his chest. "Good to know you enjoy it." He met my eyes. "I feel bad that you gave me that, and I can't do anything for you back."

"Well, it's not like I'm keeping score, you know. I did it because I wanted to. You came to visit me, and I can't tell you how much that means to me. I know you're insane with this tour, so I know how much it took to take the time away." I smirked at him. "But if you're that worried, you can just keep a tally of how many orgasms I give you, and when I'm cleared for sex, you can pay me back."

Chase nodded seriously. "Okay, then. A tally system it is." He dug his phone out of his hip pocket, swiped it open, and tapped the yellow *notepad* app.

I laughed as he wrote "Orgasm Tally Card" on the top line. He spaced down a line and wrote the numeral 1 on the next. "I was actually joking, Chase. It's not a who's-come-the-most competition, babe."

"It is now." He pushed his phone back into his pocket. "So how have you been passing the time, my love?"

I laughed again, this time more in deprecation. "Poorly. I'm bored out of my fucking skull, Chase. I'm restless. Antsy. I've never spent this much time being lazy in my life."

"It's not laziness, Jay." Chase squeezed me against his side. "It's doctor-ordered bed rest. You're the least lazy woman I know."

"Nice try, babe, but that's not how it feels to me." I sighed. "All I do is sit on my ass, watching Netflix and knitting."

Chase guffawed. "Knitting? You? Since when do you *knit*?"

I frowned at him. "Why couldn't I knit? Maybe you just didn't know I did."

He rolled his eyes. "You don't knit, Jay. You just don't. No more than I do."

I glared at him, more offended than I had a right to be, since my reaction when Kelly first suggested it wasn't too far from Chase's. "I do too knit. Now, at least." I reached over the side of the couch and set my knitting bag on his lap.

A stunned expression on his face, he rummaged in the bag, pulling out my pillow/case hat, the holey scarf of shitty knitting, and my latest project, one sock out of the pair for Chase. "Damn, Jay, you *have* been knitting." He held up the pillowcase/hat, clearing his throat in an effort to not laugh. "Um...honey? What is this?"

I snatched it from him. "Shut up, you. It's a hat. Or a pillowcase. It can be both, if it wants to."

Chase took it back and set it on his head. His entire face was obscured by the multicolored yarn. "A hat?"

I snatched it off his head. "For a Rasta. To cover his dreads."

Chase laughed harder. "Do you even know any Rastas? And he'd have to have, like, the biggest, longest, thickest dreads ever for this thing to fit."

I smashed it onto his head and pulled it down over his face. "Shut up. It was the first thing I tried making. I've only been doing this for, like, a week." I grabbed a square throw pillow and stuffed it into the hat; it fit, barely, and the corners poked through the holes, stretching it to ridiculous proportions. "It's harder than you might think."

"I'm not making fun of you, baby. I promise. It's just...it's funny." Chase pulled out the scarf next and wrapped it around his neck, posing and batting his eyelashes. "Does it go with my outfit?"

"Now you're just being a dick." I took the bag from him and dug in it until I found the one sock I'd finished. "I did make you something, but you probably don't want it now, since I'm such a crappy knitter."

Chase laughed and kissed the nape of my neck, knowing how that melted me. "I do want it, baby. I'm just teasing. I'm sorry."

I handed him the sock. "It's a sock. I've only finished one."

Chase's face twisted in his effort to not laugh. "Um. It's a sock?" He coughed, trying gamely to keep a straight face. "A sock for me?"

He unlaced his boot and tugged it off, then held the sock up to his foot. I had to hold back a snicker myself as I saw the thing I'd made against his foot. The sock was a cylindrical tube, and it was clear he wouldn't be able to get even part of his foot into it. It was too narrow across the opening and wouldn't even cover his heel, even if he could get it on.

I bit my lip as Chase nonetheless tried to lever his foot into the "sock." He managed his big toe and the one next to it.

Then genius struck.

"It's not a sock for your foot, honey." I kept a straight face, miraculously.

"It's not?" He peered at me in confusion.

"Nope."

"Then what—" He broke off as I glanced at his crotch, a smirk on my lips. "No. No way."

"Yep. It's a cock sock." I choked on my laughter.

"You're full of shit," Chase said. "You did *not* make me a cock sock."

"I did, too. Look at it. It's just big enough to fit on that third leg of yours." I reached for his pants. "Try it on. Come on, baby, model that cock sock for me."

Chase buried his face in his hands. "No. Uh-uh. No way."

"Yes! You have to! I want to see how it fits." I fought his hands away and managed to unzip him, freeing his cock.

Chase sighed theatrically and stood up, his pants open and hanging loose. He snatched the sock from me with a glare and slid it onto his cock, but it didn't quite fit yet. "It's too big, honey."

"It'll fit when you're hard," I said, taking his yarn-clad cock in my hands and caressing him into erection. When he was fully hard, the sock fit perfectly. "See?"

Chase waggled his hips so his shaft waved side to side, the green, orange, and white sock tight around his turgid cock. "The latest in men's fashion...the cock sock!" He strutted from one side of the living room, hands on his hips, mimicking a catwalk sway until his pants fell around his ankles.

I laughed so hard I stopped breathing, gasping and snorting. "Stop, stop, oh, god!"

"It's quite comfortable," he remarked, waving his cock in my face. "I think it'll be great for keeping my cock warm when I get morning wood."

"What the *fuck* is going on?" Kelly's voice screeched from the kitchen doorway. "Oh, my god. I'm scarred for life. Chase Michael Delany, put some goddamned pants on before I have to rip out my eyeballs!"

I had just calmed down, but Kelly's surprise appearance into our little fashion show and Chase's mortified reaction sent me into paroxysms of laughter once more. I watched Chase tug his pants on and button them hurriedly, the cock sock still on.

"Don't you work until four, Mom?" Chase said, tugging the sock out of his pants.

Kelly made a grimace of disgust. "Oh, my god. I'm going to have nightmares for the rest of my life." She turned away from us both, scrubbing her face with her hands. "There was a scheduling mess-up, so I got sent home early. Jesus, seriously, what were you two doing? Jamie can't have sex, Chase, surely you know that."

"Yes, Mom, I know that." He lifted the sock. "Jamie knitted a sock for me, but it didn't fit my foot—"

"La-la-la! Not listening!" Kelly yelled, covering her ears. "Forget I asked. I don't want to know. I really, *really* don't want to know."

"I'm sorry you saw that, Mom."

"I'll just have that image burned into my brain forever, no big deal." She pinched the bridge of her nose while Chase and I exchanged glances and tried not to laugh. "It's good you're here, though, Chase. Jamie has a doctor's appointment tomorrow morning. You can come."

He nodded. "My flight out isn't until the day after tomorrow, so that'll work."

I woke up the next day with a headache so bad I didn't want to get out of bed. The sunlight streaming in through the window was too bright, piercing my closed eyes and making my head throb even worse. I heard the door squeak open, and smelled coffee and toast.

"I brought you breakfast, baby," Chase said, settling onto the bed next to me.

"My head hurts so bad, Chase. Can you close the blinds for me?" My voice sounded tiny, hesitant and weak. I hurt too bad to care.

"Yeah, sure," he said, getting up to slide the blinds closed. "You want some Tylenol?"

"Please. Regular extra-strength Tylenol."

He came back, and I heard Kelly's light tread behind his. "Your head hurts, Jamie?"

"Yeah. Really, really bad. A migraine, I think. I get them sometimes. I haven't had one in a long time, though."

Kelly didn't answer right away, which worried me. "Why don't you let Chase help you get dressed? We should head to Dr. Rayburn's office."

I peered from beneath the blanket at the clock, which read eight-fifteen in the morning. "I thought the appointment was at eleven?"

"It is," Kelly said, "but the headache isn't a good sign. I'd rather get you checked out earlier."

I was almost twenty-eight weeks at that point, and looked like someone had stuffed a beach ball under my skin. I let Chase help me dress, which was awkward and embarrassing, and then rode in the back seat of Kelly's car to the doctor's office. Tests, pee in a cup (so incredibly fun *that* is), more tests...oh, and Mrs. Delany, can you please collect your urine every time you pee for the next twenty-four hours?

Um, I pee every six seconds. I'll need a fucking vat to put all the pee in at that rate. But it's for the baby's wellness and my own, so in a cup I pee...every six seconds. It's every bit as exciting as it sounds, and infinitely more messy than you can possibly believe.

Chase pushed his flight back till the afternoon and went back in to see Dr. Rayburn with me in the morning. Marcia Rayburn was a short, svelte, older woman with steel-gray hair, quick-witted and no-nonsense.

"I think I'm going to admit you to the hospital, Jamie. Your protein levels are really high. That, combined with the headaches and the back and shoulder pain? I'm going to need to observe you for a few days. If your levels don't go down, we might need to look at an induction earlier than I'd originally planned." Dr. Rayburn offered me a reassuring smile that seemed at odds with her foreboding words.

"For a few days?" I said, my voice catching at the end. "Like, how many days?"

"Three or four? It depends on how things go." Dr. Rayburn clicked her pen in and out.

"Worst-case scenario," Chase said. "How early would you need to deliver the baby?"

Dr. Rayburn didn't answer right away. "I can't say with any degree of accuracy. It all depends. Jamie has reported some changes in her vision, which, along with the headache today, could mean she's at risk for eclampsia, or seizures, or at the least severe preeclampsia. If her symptoms worsen to any significant degree, we would need to deliver immediately. Obviously we want her to go closer to full term, or at least thirty-two or thirty-four weeks. Thirty-six would be best, but I don't really see that happening, honestly."

"If you have to deliver this soon, what would happen?" Chase's voice was heavy with worry.

"Well, it would be a premature birth, obviously. At twenty-eight or twenty-nine weeks, the baby would require an extended stay in the NICU, as her lungs would likely not be totally viable yet. There are a lot of factors, and honestly, I don't want to worry you with them needlessly until we're sure it's going to come to that, and it very well may not." Dr. Rayburn tucked the pen into the pocket of her lab coat and stood up. "I'd like you to pick up a home blood pressure cuff and monitor your blood pressure as well. If you notice any increase at all, and I mean at *all*, call the emergency line for my office and have them page me. If the increase is significant, go straight to the hospital. Same thing for the other symptoms. If your headache worsens, if your vision changes at all, or if the back or shoulder pain worsens, go to the hospital. Don't dismiss it or try to tough it out. Okay?"

I nodded and tried to swallow my panic. "Sure, whatever you say."

She patted my knee. "It's going to be okay, Jamie. I promise. We'll take care of you and the baby. Don't stress yourself out with games of what-if, okay? That's important. You need to rest and relax and be calm."

I laughed, somewhat mirthlessly. "I'll try, Doc, but this is stressful. I'm worried. The what-ifs are running rampant already, and I'm not even alone yet."

Dr. Rayburn just nodded and opened the door, pausing to look over her shoulder. "Mr. Delany, I understand your band requires constant travel, but I must stress how vital to her well-being—and that of your baby—your presence is. Call her, text her, Skype her, visit her as often as possible. You simply cannot know how much your mere presence will help her. I implore you to make every effort to see her as much as possible."

Chase nodded, his expression unreadable, which meant to me that he was seriously stressed. "I understand, Doctor. Thank you."

We left the office in silence and drove home in silence, the radio off for once. We pulled into Kelly's driveway and Chase turned off the car, but didn't move to get out.

"I love my job," he said, staring out the window. "I love being in a band. I love making music. I love the crowds, I love the attention. The guys... they're my brothers, you know? There's nothing else I'd rather spend my life doing. But this? God, it's impossible. It's fucking...fucking impossible. I need to be here with you. I *need* to. I can't sleep at night worrying about you. I lie in the bunk on the bus and stare at the ceiling, wondering if you're okay, if Samantha's okay. I play the set, I sing my goddamn heart out every night, but I'm not there on stage. I'm on autopilot—the rest of me is here. With you."

I squeezed my eyes shut, knowing me breaking down was not what he needed right then. "You're doing what you have to do, babe. I know that. It's hard without you—I'm not gonna lie about that. It's fucking hard, and I miss you. But don't think for one second that I regret anything, that I hold it against you or resent you, or your job."

Chase finally looked at me. His eyes were a study in complexity, at once tender and hurting and loving and molten and determined. "Thank you, Jamie. That's...you don't know how bad I needed to hear that." He took my hand in his and simply held it, threading his fingers through mine. "I'm not sure I can stay away. I'm going crazy. I'm burning out. I haven't—haven't really talked to anyone about this, and I hate that I'm adding to your stress, but I have to vent. I'm starting to hate the tour. I'm cranky. I'm snapping. I'm—I'm drinking alone in my room after shows, just to dull the edge of my worry. I just have this pit of fear in my stomach that something's going to happen while I'm on the fucking tour and I won't be able to get there in—in time."

I had never seen Chase so distraught. He scrubbed his hand through his hair again and again until it was wild. His hands squeezed around the steering wheel so hard I heard the material squeaking under his grip. I touched his shoulder, hesitantly at first, and then, when he flinched before leaning toward me, I leaned across the console to pull him into a hug. I put my lips to the shell of his ear, nuzzling him.

"You only have a few more shows, honey. Call me every night, okay? Fall asleep on the phone with me. Don't drink, please? Don't go there. Call me. Even if we don't talk, just be with me on the phone. I know it's hard, and I—I won't lie and say I don't wish you were able to just cut the tour short, but that has to be the absolute last resort. But it won't come to that. I'll get to thirty-two weeks, at least. You have to finish the tour. I know it, and you know it. The guys are counting on you."

Chase nodded, his face buried in my shoulder. "I know. I just hate it." He pulled away and rubbed the heels of his hands into his eye sockets. "Thank god for Mom, huh? I'd be out of a job for sure if you were stuck alone in New York for all this."

I laughed. "No shit."

Chase glanced at his phone, then slammed his hand into the steering wheel. "Fuck. I have to go. My flight out is in less than three hours." Chase leaned in and kissed me, slowly and thoroughly. It was a farewell kiss, and I was crying by the end of it. "If you cry, I won't be able to leave."

I sniffled and wiped my eyes, summoned the dregs of my courage and shoved the selfish sadness down, ran my hand through his soft black hair and kissed his cheekbone. "Go. I love you. Call me." I got out of Chase's rental car and backed away. "Go be a rock star, baby."

He smiled sadly. "I'd rather be here being a husband and daddy."

"Soon. Go." I waved at him, one hand on my belly.

What I hadn't told him was that I had the same sense of foreboding, a feeling that my three or four days in the hospital would turn in to an emergency C-section and Chase would miss it, and I'd be alone in the O.R., trying not to cry.

I rubbed my belly. "Stay in there for me, Sam. Okay?" I felt a flutter, and then a foot or elbow pushed against my hand, eliciting a laugh. "Be a good girl for me and stay in there until Daddy can be with us. Please?"

Chapter 5: Anna

Our OB, Dr. Michaela Irving, paused for a terrifyingly long moment before delivering the news. "You're measuring a little over three weeks behind where you should be, Anna. Both twins are small, worrisomely so." She glanced at the papers in the file folder, more to gather her thoughts, I guessed, than for any actual information.

I struggled with accepting her news. "What? I'm eating healthier than ever before in my entire life. I'm—I'm doing everything I can, I swear! I don't—I don't get it."

Dr. Irving held up her hands to stop me. "Anna, it's got nothing to do with what you're doing or what you're eating. You're doing everything right. Sometimes these things just happen, especially with twins. I know I've explained the risks associated with having twins—well, this is one more that exists. You're thirty-one weeks tomorrow, and I'd like you to make it to thirty-four, if possible. We'll have to have you in to measure your progress at least once a week, but if I don't see sufficient progress, I'm going to schedule an induction. A lot of my colleagues will only do a C-section for twins, but I'd like you to try to deliver naturally if you can."

"I'd like to deliver naturally, too," I said. "But whatever you think is safest for the babies."

Dr. Irving stood. "Just stay positive and keep doing what you're doing. See Tasha on the way out and schedule an ultrasound for next week, 'kay?"

I just nodded and squeezed Jeff's hand. He'd been silent for the entire ultrasound and Dr. Irving's prognosis. "I'm scared, Jeff."

He didn't respond immediately. "It'll be okay. Just—we'll just take it one day at a time, one ultrasound at a time."

The next week, Jeff had a gig DJing a blow-out Bat Mitzvah in Bloomfield Hills that was paying too much money to ignore, so I went to the ultrasound alone. I had progressed some, but Dr. Irving still seemed more worried than she was saying. She had me come in three days later, rather than the next week, which had me in a panic. At my thirty-third-week ultrasound, Dr. Irving again remained silent for several minutes.

"You're still measuring far enough behind that I'm worried the babies aren't getting what they need. It's always a balancing act with twins, especially in situations like this. Obviously the farther along you're able to go, the better it is for the babies, but with twins, it always gets more complicated. With your measurements and the rate of progression I'm seeing, my feeling is that it would be best to induce you next week."

I twisted the strap of my purse between my fingers. "Are they...will they both be viable?"

"I believe so," she replied. "I'm the most worried about the boy, since he's measuring smaller than his sister. Their lungs both look good, though, so I'm very optimistic."

I hated that phrase. *Very optimistic.* Like she was discussing the weather for an upcoming ball game or something, rather than the lives of my babies. I didn't express this, though. I just nodded and squeezed Jeff's hand so hard he frowned at me. He was, as he'd been through most of the appointments, silent, watchful, a solid presence beside me, calming me as much as possible.

On the way home, I turned to Jeff. "Can we swing by Kelly's house? I want to see Jamie." He just nodded, staring straight ahead. "Talk to me, Jeff. I can feel you stewing over there."

He frowned at me. "I'm not stewing."

"You've barely spoke three words to me all week," I said.

"What do you want me to say?" He jabbed the radio off with an impatient stab of his thumb.

"I don't know. Anything. I mean, I know you're a man of few words, but this is ridiculous."

That got a chuckle from him, but he quickly sobered. "I'm worried, Anna. Is that what you want to hear? I'm scared for you, and for our babies. You're gonna deliver six weeks early? Isn't that, like, a fucking lot? And she's having you do a vaginal birth when just about every other doctor in the field recommends a C-section for twin births? What if she's wrong? What if something goes wrong?" He swung around a corner too fast, and hit the gas until we were going so fast I clutched the handle with white knuckles. "What if—what if...god, there's so much going through my mind I don't know where to even start, so I just—don't. I keep it in, because you're worried, too—you're scared, too, and you need me to be the strong one, the calm one."

"Slow down, Jeff, you're scaring me." He took his foot off the accelerator and we slowed down enough that I could relax. "Like I said, you're stewing. We're both scared, Jeff. We've never done this before. Yeah, I need you to be my rock like you always are, but I also need you to talk to me. You do me no good if you're lost in your own head.

You may as well not even be here if you're gonna do that."

"I don't know how to deal with all this, Anna. It's so much. There's so many elements to this, so many factors, so many ways it could go wrong, and I'd—I'd lose you. Lose the babies. I can't—"

I took his hand and kissed his palm. "That's not going to happen, honey. Nothing's going to go wrong. Dr. Irving knows what she's doing. I trust her. No one is going to lose anyone."

He smiled at me, but it didn't entirely reach his eyes. "Just—I love you. And I'm worried. That's all."

"It's going to be fine, baby."

"Why are you the one comforting me here?" He laughed, tangling our fingers together and bringing my knuckle to his lips. "It's going to be fine."

"It's going to be fine," I agreed. He pulled into Kelly Delany's driveway, and I stopped him before he shut the truck off. "Why don't you go out and have a drink or something? Relax. Have some alone time."

He seemed baffled by the idea. "A drink? At two o'clock in the afternoon on a Tuesday?"

"Or whatever. I'm not saying go get hammered. Just go and relax, and let me have some time with Jay."

He nodded. "There's a shooting range not far from here. Maybe I'll got shoot some rounds."

I kissed him and made my way to the front door, where Jamie was already waiting, waving at Jeff as he backed out.

"Hey, hooker," I said, hugging her, our bellies bumping as we awkwardly tried to maneuver in for a proper embrace. "You look great!"

Jamie snorted. "Shut up, you lying sack of shit. I look like fucking Shamu at this point. Except Shamu can jump through a hoop, and I can barely get my ass off the damn couch to take a piss."

I laughed. "Well, I'm finally catching up to you in the whale department. We're about the same size now."

She stood beside me, and we compared bellies. "Except you're almost two weeks farther along than I am. And you have twins."

My smile faded a bit. "Yeah, well, that's why my doctor wants to induce me next week."

Jamie frowned and took my hand in hers. "Really? Mine, too."

"I thought she said things were looking better?"

Jamie shrugged. "Yeah, well, not anymore. After being basically chained to a hospital bed for three days, my protein count and blood pressure had leveled off a bit, but now they're back up and worse than ever. She's not sure I'll make it to next week. I'm supposed to go in tomorrow to get checked."

"Sorry I couldn't come see you while you were in the hospital, hon. We had that gig in Jackson, and then I had an ultrasound that just took forever and I was so tired by the end—"

Jamie clapped her hand over my mouth. "It's fine, Anna. You already explained. It really wasn't that bad. I had wifi and my iPad and my knitting. I just hate hospitals. You have to stay in bed and wait and wait and wait for absolutely nothing. And then they tell you, 'oh, we'll check on you in a couple hours,' but really they mean like, some time the next week they *might* remember to come back."

I laughed. "Yeah, not looking forward to that."

"So we'll be having our babies together, huh?" Jamie handed me a caffeine-free diet Coke—gross—and we sat on the couch together.

We both burst out laughing when we approached the process of sitting down the same way: bracing one hand on the arm of the couch, leaning forward into a sitting position as we lowered ourselves to the cushions, easing down until our leg muscles couldn't support our weight any longer, and then falling the rest of the way.

"I guess we will," I said, hand on my belly to feel a little foot kick-kicking away so hard it took my breath away. "Jeez, kid, take it easy," I said, looking down at my stomach.

Jamie laid her hand where mine was, and I moved her palm over slightly so she could feel the kicking. "Damn, that kid can kick!"

"I know!" I winced as the other baby started in on the other side of my belly.

"Do you know which one that is?" Jamie asked.

"I think Caleb is on the left, Niall on the right."

"So that's Niall kicking you over here, then." She had her palm on the right side of my belly, where Niall was trying to punt her way out, it felt like.

"Pretty sure that's where they were last ultrasound."

Jamie laid her head back on the couch and looked at me sideways. "Are you ready, Anna?"

I mirrored her pose. "Hell, no. I'm not ready for *one* baby, much less two. I never thought I'd be a mom, you know? Even after I started dating Jeff, I didn't really think it'd happen. Not that I didn't want it to, I just…I don't know. I never really let on to Jeff, but I was, and still am, scared I won't be a good mom."

Jamie sighed, and it sounded like relief. "God, thank you. I thought that was just me. Sometimes, despite feeling her kick and, like, *knowing* there's a baby in there, I don't really feel like this is real. Am I really about to have an actual human being squirt out of my hoo-ha? For actual-factual real? A little human being that's going to be completely dependent on me? What if I fuck up?"

I laughed. "I think there won't be a lot of actual squirting, Jay. I think it's going to be more screaming and trying to shit, from what I've seen on *A Baby Story*."

"You watch that, too? I hate it, but I can't stop watching. I keep thinking it'll help me be ready for actually giving birth, but then all it does is freak me out even worse."

I took a sip from the flat, watery-tasting caffeine-free Diet Coke and tried not to grimace at it...in vain. "We're not gonna be shitty moms, are we, Jay?"

Jamie sighed, staring out the window at a robin hopping across the lawn. "I fucking hope not. I mean, there's no real manual for this shit, you know? All the self-help books and TV shows and *What to Expect When You're Expecting*...all that won't make a difference when it comes time to actually have the baby, to actually be a mother. Doesn't stop me from reading it all and watching it all, hoping it'll help or something. But I know, deep down, once the baby comes...everything is going to change. And all you can do is hope you're able to figure it out as it all happens."

I groaned. "Damn Jay, that's pessimistic as all hell."

"Well, do you have a better way of looking at it? 'Cause I'd love to hear it."

I watched carbonation bubble up and stick to the sides of the glass rather than meet Jay's eyes.

"Not really, I guess. I think I'm more hoping that, like, I'll just know what to do when the time comes, you know? I mean, is anyone ever really prepared to be a parent? No, but also yes. I mean, it's part of the human cycle, you know? It's programmed into us, into our genes or DNA or whatever, to reproduce and to take care of our offspring. Not everyone is the same, and some people are more suited to parenthood than others. I mean, look at my parents. They were shitty parents. But I'm determined to love my kids and take care of them the way I wish my parents had me."

Jamie nodded. "Exactly my feelings. I may not get any 'Mom of the Year' awards, but at least I'll be better than *my* folks were."

I watched as the corners of Jamie's eyes tightened, as if from pain. "Are you all right?"

"Yeah, just a headache."

"*Jamie*. Didn't your doctor tell you not to just ignore a headache? Especially at this stage?"

"God, Anna. Yes, yes, you're right. But—"

"But nothing." I levered myself to my feet. "Are you packed?"

"Packed?" She gave me a panicked look. "Packed for what?"

I called Jeff, ignoring Jamie's squawks of protest. "Hey, baby. You can come get us now."

"'Us'? Referring to yourself in the plural, now, are we?"

I snorted. "No, it's Jamie who does that. But Jamie's got another headache, and I'm making her go in to the hospital."

"Oh," he said, and I heard the sounds of pistols in the background fading as he left the range. "I'll be there in ten."

Jamie sat on the couch, glaring at me as I slid the phone into my purse again. "Anna, seriously—"

"No, you seriously. Quit fighting me on this. You know you have to." I grabbed both of her hands and pulled her upright, then smacked her ass as she shuffled toward her bedroom. "Now go get your hospital bag and let's go."

"Fine. Hooker."

"Stubborn-ass ho."

The fact that she didn't put up more of a fight told me what I needed to know. The increasing tension around her eyes and the way she clenched her jaw as she slid into the back seat gave me enough of a clue that I knew I was doing the right thing.

When we were nearly to the hospital, I turned around to look at her. "Should you call Chase?"

She shook her head. "Not yet. Not until I hear what the doctors have to say."

After a couple hours' wait, and a battery of tests later, she was officially admitted to William Beaumont Hospital's Labor and Delivery unit. She called Chase.

Samantha Delany was on her way.

Bridge

CHASE WAS UNEASY. He was backstage waiting for Six Foot Tall to go on. Device, David Draiman's new band, was on, finishing their last set, and they were killing. It was Draiman, though, so of course they killed. Disturbed was a huge influence on Chase's harder music, so the opportunity to play with David Draiman last minute in Chicago was a dream come true. He was geeked, nervous, a bit star-struck, and on top of it all, the down-deep fear that something was wrong was growing.

He was edgy, bouncing on his toes, cracking his knuckles over and over again, checking his silenced phone in the back pocket of his signature leather pants. He knew he needed to get his shit together, but he just couldn't shake the jitters, the sinking feeling in the pit of his stomach. He'd nearly called Jamie at least six times, but never had.

Now, he didn't have time. Device had already done a three-song encore, and Six Foot Tall was set to go on within minutes of Device leaving the stage, which had been curtained off toward the back so the next band's equipment could be set up.

"Thank you, Chicago! Good night!" David waved one last time to the screaming crowd, hometown for him, and left the stage, handing the mic to a stagehand and accepting a hand towel and a bottle of water, and was gone before Chase could open his mouth. Device had originally been slated to play a small acoustic set in a club as a soft launch for their newest tour, but the gig had been cancelled at the last minute. Then the local band that was supposed to open for Six Foot Tall had cancelled, citing an OD'd lead singer, and Device had agreed to fill the slot. Of course, David Draiman was a huge draw, so they'd taken up nearly half of Six Foot Tall's original time. Chase didn't really care, and the fans loved it. They'd just have to go overtime, which shouldn't be a problem.

The stage was cleared and reset, and Chase prepared to go on. He took a deep breath, let it out, shook his hand, then trotted out onstage. The crowd went wild as the spotlight hit him. Johnny Hawk hit the kick drum a few times, and Gage thumped his bass, setting up a rumbling line as the band got settled in.

Blue stage lights bathed him, then turned purple. He felt the nerves leave him as Kyle fingered the opening chords to their latest hit, "Shadow Thrall." Performing was the only time he felt any kind of peace lately. When the chorus came with the shrieking guitar solo underlaid by the scudding bass line, Chase was crouching at the edge of the stage, howling the lyrics: "The shadows hold me in their thrall, I cannot deny their call, I'm falling, falling, and I cannot stop this fall…"

Even then, though, the fear remained. It ate at him, dug under his skin and made his heart thump crazily, made his stomach roil and constrict. The next song fit his mood. It was their hardest metal piece to date, and it written entirely by Gage. The lyrics were dark, darker and harder than anything Chase had ever penned, but his fear gave him the edge needed to sell them.

The lights dropped to black, and Gage took front and center stage, bathed in a single red stage light. He held his black bass guitar vertically against his body, his long, fine blond hair loose around his face, obscuring his features. The crowd was silent except for a few isolated whistles and shrieks, and Gage milked it, thumping the lowest string with his thumb in a reverberating tone that washed across the audience. When the tension was thick enough to cut, he began to slowly ramp up the speed of his hammering thumb until the waves of basso reverberation were crashing back on themselves, reaching a crescendo. When the peak hit and he couldn't tap any faster, his back arched and the bass resting on his chest, he slammed forward and let loose with a thundering series of chords, headbanging to the punishing rhythm. As the rhythm reached a crescendo, Johnny began pelting the snare drums in a stuttering march pattern. When their rhythms synched, Kyle wove a repeating series of riffs through the wall of sound created by Johnny and Gage.

Then it was Chase's turn. He had slunk into the shadows near the side of the stage to accept a guitar and returned to stand between Kyle and Gage, waiting until the song hit a second crescendo and paused in single beat of silence. When sound returned, Chase added a driving backbone rhythm pattern. By now, all four members of the band were bathed in lights and the song was in full force, the crowd jumping and moshing with wild abandon.

Chase gradually moved toward the mic stand as the song progressed toward the first verse and began growling the lyrics to "Ablation":

> *Down this dirty hole*
> *You and me we crawl*
> *Through this recurring nightmare*
> *Of me against you*
> *Rage against recrimination*

Blame against damnation
Domination of my past
Versus ablation of my heart
Your nails on my spine
Was once erotic
Your eyes on mine
Was once hypnotic
But this nightmare
The way it flares
Ignites into hatred
Slices through the skin
Of your demonic beauty
Revealing the evil within
This recurring nightmare
Of me against you
Rage against recrimination
Blame against damnation
Your lies ablate my hope
Your betrayal perpetrates my hate
You were once erotic
Hypnotic
Now you're just demonic
Chthonic
A chronic cyclonic storm
Wrecking all my dreams.

Chase's voice was raw by the end of the song, by the time he'd screamed the chorus through three more times. He knew he'd sold it. He'd given in to every fear and nagging worry and put it all into the song, let it feed the lyrics with all his inner darkness. He stood in the pool of white spotlights, sweat dribbling down the shell of his ear and into the gauged hole of his piercing, heart hammering, stomach clenching, adrenaline pumping. The instruments around him all fell silent, and he forced himself to breathe through it, ignore the fear that was quickly turning into unreasoning terror.

Then his phone buzzed. He ignored it until the lights doused between songs, then spun around and dug it out of his pocket, shielding the glow with his body.

The name across the screen made his heart stutter and stop. *Jay*.

What was he supposed to do? She knew he was performing tonight. She wouldn't call him unless it was an emergency, but Johnny was already clicking his sticks to count in the next song, and the lights were up.

He shoved the phone back in his pocket and forced himself through the next song. He felt his phone buzz again, and almost lost his place in the lyrics. When the song ended, he edged up to Gage and Kyle and told them to do a solo or something, an instrumental piece to buy him time.

Chase left the stage and stood under the light of an emergency-exit sign with his phone clutched in his trembling fist.

"Hey, guys, I'm Gage. We're, uh, we're gonna do an instrumental song for you guys. It doesn't really have a name, it's just a jam we put together. Hope you like it." He heard Gage's bass kick in a fast rhythm, and then the other guys came in.

You wouldn't know they were making it all up as they went along. They'd never done an all-instrumental number before, hadn't practiced it or written it or jammed out to even have an idea. But it was buying him time, and that's all that mattered.

He pulled up the text message. *Hey, babe. I know you're onstage, sorry. It's time. The headache came back, and I've been admitted to L and D. They're gonna start a pitocin drip around midnight to induce labor. I need you here.*

Midnight. Fuck. That was in three hours. He was in Chicago, four hours away. There were no flights out till morning. He didn't have a car. The band was only three songs into an eleven-song set.

He swore again under his breath and typed a response, a promise he didn't know how to fulfill: *I'll be there. I promise.*

Gage came out to get him. "Come on, dude, you're on. 'Long Night Gone' is up next."

He met Gage's gaze. "They're inducing her in three hours, Gage. I gotta be there."

"What's that mean?"

"It means they're forcing her to go into labor early. It means she's having the baby, like, now."

"Fuck." Gage flipped his hair back from his face with an angry motion. "Fuck. What are you gonna do?"

Chase shook his head. "I don't know. I don't fucking know, man."

"Problem?" Darrel McKay said. Darrel was the lead singer for Blood Oath, a local Chicago metal band that had been the pre-opener.

"I'm about to have a baby, and I'm here. She's in Detroit. We're not even halfway through our show." Chase rubbed his hand over his head, again and again. "I don't know what to do."

"I can fill in. I don't know your material, but we can do some covers." Darrel ran his fingers through his shoulder-length black hair, flipping it back.

"That works for me," Gage said. "Let's do it. You make the announcement, Chase, and then get going."

Chase shook hands and bumped fists with his band-mates, and then took the stage, sitting on the very edge with his feet hanging off. He lifted the mic to his lips, shaded his eyes against the glare of the stage lights and the spot bathing him. "So, hey, Chicago. How's it going? Having a good time?" The crowd cheered and applauded until Chase lifted a hand to silence them. "Some of you may know I got married a little while back, and my wife is expecting a baby."

There was more applause, a few boos from the disappointed female members of the audience, and some shouts of congratulations.

"So, the reason I'm sitting here like this, talking to you rather than singing the next song, is that I just got a text from Jamie, my wife, and she just went into labor." He paused and scratched his head. "Well, actually, she's getting induced, if you want to get technical, but that's beside the point. The point is, I have to go witness the birth of my daughter. This is—and you have to believe me— this is the *only* reason I would ever leave in the middle of a concert. I hate doing this, I really do. You guys are the reason I'm here, the reason the boys and I are able to live our dream like we have been."

He stood up, waved to the other guys, and took center stage. "So, you guys paid good money to hear us play, and just because he's a badass, David has graciously offered to kind of fill in for me. So, is anyone here a fan of Blood Oath?" The crowd screamed wildly for the local talent, and it was several long moments before anyone could be heard over the noise. "I take it that means you'll let us change things on you? The guys from Six Foot Tall are gonna play, and Darrel is gonna sing, and I personally think Darrel is fucking badass. They'll rock your shit, I guarantee you. They might even take a couple requests."

Darrel lifted the mic to his lips. "Hey, you're about to have a kid, man. It's the least I could do to help a brother out." He pushed Chase toward the side of the stage. "Now go, get the fuck out of here and be with your wife."

"If you follow me on Twitter or Facebook, check for updates. Thank you, Chicago!" Chase waved to the crowd and left the stage as the band kicked in the opening notes to "Down With the Sickness" in tribute to David Draiman, who was watching from backstage.

Less than half an hour later, Chase was in a car borrowed from a roadie and flying as fast as he could safely drive toward Detroit. The fear in his belly had faded a bit but hadn't gone away completely.

Something told him the insanity had just started.

Wait for me, Samantha, he thought. *Wait for me.*

Chapter 6: Jamie

A LONG, GROWLING GROAN ripped from my throat, a sound of frustration, pain, and panic. The OB on duty, Dr. Clayton, had ordered a pitocin drip to start labor, but the anesthesiologist hadn't shown up yet, despite the passage of more than two hours, so I was feeling the full force of every contraction, and they were increasing in intensity with every half hour.

Chase still wasn't here, and all I'd heard from him was a single text an hour before: *OTW, driving now, be there soon.*

Anna and Jeff had gone home, at my insistence; I knew it would be several hours before anything happened, and they had Anna's complicated pregnancy to deal with. I was, once again, alone and in pain. I breathed in through my nose as a contraction gripped my core and squeezed. It felt like a menstrual cramp amplified by a million. I whimpered, trying to breathe through it, counting in my head, *One-one thousand...two-one thousand...three-one thousand...four-one thousand...*and then it passed, leaving me slumped back against the thin pillow, sweating and panting.

"Where the fuck is the drugs man?" I growled to the empty room at large.

A nurse breezed in at that moment and checked the charts and beeping monitors, adjusted the fitting of the circular monitor pickup strapped to my belly. "He's coming, hon. Another patient had a complication with her epidural."

"A complication?" My voice squeaked at the end, panicking at the idea of a complication happening to me.

"Nothing for you to worry about, dear." The nurse was a young brunette with wide brown eyes and an easy smile. "Just a slightly-off placement is all. You'll be just fine. Dr. Harris is an excellent doctor. You have nothing to worry about, I promise."

"God, don't scare me like that. I'm freaked out enough as it is." I sucked on the straw in my miniature can of Vernor's.

"Do you have anyone here with you, Mrs. Delany?" the nurse asked.

"Yeah, my friends just left, and my husband is on the way."

"Where's he coming from?"

I felt my womb tensing in preparation for another contraction. "Chicago—he actually left in the middle of a show."

The nurse scanned the printout coming from the monitor, assessing the frequency and intensity of the contractions. "Oh? What does he do?"

I laughed. "You must be the only nurse in the whole L and D who doesn't know." I gritted my teeth and breathed through the contraction, then exhaled in relief when it passed. "My husband is Chase Delany from Six Foot Tall."

I could tell the nurse tried to contain her excitement, but she wasn't entirely successful. "Oh, my god! I love them! I saw them at Harpos before they blew up!"

"Well, you'll meet him as soon as he gets his ass here." I took another sip from my soda and then crunched an ice chip, wishing desperately for something other than ice and soda.

"Did he really leave in the middle of a concert to be with you?" the nurse asked, clearly awed.

"That's what I hear. I haven't actually talked to him yet, but I know he's supposed to be playing right now, and instead he's driving to get here."

"Well, things seem to be progressing pretty quickly, especially since this is your first baby. It'll still be several hours more before the baby gets here, if everything happens like it should." She turned to leave, pausing at the door. "Dr. Clayton should be here to check how far you've progressed in a little while, and Dr. Henry should be along with the epidural any minute."

"Awesome," I muttered, thinking about how large Dr. Clayton's hands had been when he'd first checked me upon admittance to the L and D ward. Large, hard, and cold.

Not a good combination when your profession was shoving your hands up the hoo-ha of unsuspecting women. There should be a requirement that all OBs have small, warm hands. Careful hands. I also thought the idea of a male OB was kind of contrary. What the hell does a man know about girly bits? He doesn't have them. Clinical knowledge only got you so far, after all.

What it amounted to was me wishing for Dr. Rayburn to get her ass to the hospital for the actual birth. She'd been paged when I had first arrived at Beaumont, but there hadn't been any word as yet. Dr. Rayburn's hands were perfect, small, gentle, sure, and not frigid. She also possessed the ability to make me feel like it would all be okay with a few calm words. There was just something about her demeanor that set me at ease.

Dr. Clayton? Not so much. He was over six feet tall, middle-aged, built like a grizzly bear, and not given to talking unless necessary. He wasn't surly or taciturn, just gruff and quiet. He really was a nice enough guy, and if he'd been any other kind of doctor, I would have been reassured by his quiet competence. As an OB/GYN, though, he put me on edge.

Speaking of whom.... Dr. Clayton strolled in at that moment, reading something on a tablet. He slid the pad in his lab coat pocket and went to the monitoring station, glancing through the contraction chart and checking the pickups for the monitor. Still without speaking, he snapped on a pair of rubber gloves, kicked the door shut, and plopped onto the rolling stool, scooting into position between my knees. He pushed the sheet up to my hips, and without so much as a preparatory how-do-you-do, slid his hand between my legs.

I winced and tried to contain my curses as he wiggled his huge finger around inside me, then sighed in relief when he withdrew his hand and stripped the gloves off. A quick hand-wash, and the doctor resumed his seat on the stool, repositioning the sheet to cover me.

"Well, Mrs. Delany, you're progressing pretty quickly, actually. You're about sixty percent effaced and dilated to almost five. You have a ways to go yet, but at this rate it shouldn't be too much longer." He scratched the salt-and-pepper stubble on his jaw and stood up. "Just sit tight for now. I'm going to leave the pitocin where it is for now, since you seem to be progressing nicely. I'll check you again in a few hours. I saw Dr. Harris just a minute ago, so that epidural is on its way."

And he was gone, just like that. I wondered why he thought it necessary to to tell me to sit tight. Like I was going anywhere? I sighed and gripped the railing as another contraction ripped through me. This one lasted longer, clenched me tighter, and left me breathless with relief when it finally passed.

In the background, Tom announced the next dancers on *Dancing With the Stars*, and I tried not to cry. I knew Chase was on his way, but that didn't help me feel any less alone in that moment.

"Come on, Chase, hurry up, baby." I hissed through my teeth as the next contraction hit me like a ton of bricks, barely five minutes after the last one.

It was another hour before the anesthesiologist showed up. Dr. Harris was an older American-Asian man with thick black hair barely contained by some kind of scrubs-hat. He helped me to a sitting position on the edge of the bed and wiped my back with iodine from the kit he'd unpackaged on the moveable table. I tried to keep my breathing even and pushed away my desperate wish for Chase's hands to hold as the needle—which looked about eight feet long—pierced through my skin and slid, cold and alien, into my spine. Sharp lances of pain shot through me with each motion of the doctor's careful hands, with each sliding inch of the needle. I held as still as I could and tried not to breathe as he inserted the line and taped it to my back with medical tape.

I couldn't stop a whimper from escaping as a contraction clutched me in a vise-like grip. Sweat beaded on my forehead and dripped down my cheek, tangling with my hair and causing strands to stick to my skin. My eyes squeezed shut, I started when I felt Dr. Harris' hands touch my shoulders as he urged me back to a lying position.

"I got it in first try," he said, touching buttons on a box attached to the IV hook of my bed. "There, the drip has started. You should feel relief almost immediately."

I whimpered again, this time in relief. Numbness spread through my lower half, cutting away the spearing pain of an onrushing contraction. I still felt pressure, but not pain. It was odd, actually. The contractions clenched me still, and I felt the vise-grip pressure around my womb, but it was pressure absent pain.

"Thank you, sweet baby Jesus." I closed my eyes and relaxed into the uncomfortable bed.

I heard the doctor chuckle as he cleaned up. Exhaustion stole over me, and I felt sleep tug me under. The contractions gripped me every few minutes, but I was able to doze off into a restless sleep. When I woke up, Chase was sitting with his elbows on the edge of the bed, worry etched on his gorgeous features.

"You're here," I mumbled, reaching for his hand.

"I'm here, finally." He scooted the chair closer, reaching out to brush a tendril of hair away from my eyes. "There was a huge accident on seventy-five, so I was stuck for a fucking hour and a half. I almost got arrested for trying to go on the shoulder around the pileup."

I laughed. "You did not, did you?"

Chase grinned. "Yeah, I did. For real. The cop only let me go when I told him who I was and why I needed to get here."

"You missed the giant needle," I said, scooting slowly and awkwardly up to a reclined sitting position. "It was seriously like a fucking sword."

"What giant needle?"

"The epidural," I said, holding my hands about two feet apart. "It was seriously, like, this big."

"Honey, it couldn't have been *that* big." Chase laughed.

I huffed. "It was, too. Six inches at least."

"Did it hurt?"

I stared at him. "I have a six-inch needle sticking out of my spine, Chase. What do you think?"

"The needle is still in?" Chase asked.

"I don't know. I don't think so, but it's not like I could see what he was doing. Yes, it hurt, but it makes the contractions bearable."

"What are the contractions like?" Chase threaded his fingers through mine and shifted in the visitor's chair.

I widened my eyes as I felt the squeeze of a contraction. I glanced at the monitor readout and saw that the contractions had ramped up significantly while I dozed. They were frequent and powerful now, the chart looking like a mountain range of peaks and valleys.

"Before the epidural they were, no lie, the most painful thing I've ever felt. I don't even know how to describe it to you. There's nothing like it, especially that a man would experience. It's like menstrual cramps, but times a million, but you don't know what that feels like." I adjusted the blanket to better cover my toes. "The best I can put it is like a giant fist squeezing your stomach. Now that I've got the epidural in, it's more like how you feel something happening when you're getting dental work done under local anesthetic. You can feel the tugging and the pressure, and it's kind of uncomfortable, but it doesn't exactly hurt, you know?"

Chase nodded. "I guess I get that." He ran a hand over his head, the already-messy black spikes getting even messier. "So what's happening? I mean, where are we, or whatever?"

I shrugged. "Just waiting, I guess."

"Waiting for what?"

"For my body to be ready to have the baby?" I reached for my cup of ice, discovering it to be empty. "Can you get me more ice? There's a little room down the hall, a pantry kind of thing. You can get something from the fridge if you want, or coffee."

"All you want it is ice?"

I rolled my eyes. "Don't get me started. If you have anything in your stomach, the epidural makes you nauseous, so you're not allowed to eat anything. It's awful. I'm so hungry, but all I can have is liquids and ice chips."

Chase stood up and leaned over me, pressing his lips to mine. "I'll be back, then."

He left, and I watched through the open door as the nurses all stared after him, whispering behind their hands. One of them glanced at me and blushed, then came in.

"That's your husband?" she asked.

I grinned. "Yeah. I know, I'm a lucky girl."

The nurse, a tiny blonde thing in the maroon scrubs of an intern, giggled. "What's it like being married to a rock star?"

I shrugged. "It's got its ups and downs. I mean, he's Chase Delany, and he's even more awesome than you can probably imagine, so there's that. But he's also gone a lot, so it's hard not being jealous of the fans that are getting more of his time and attention than me. In the seven or eight months I've been pregnant, I've seen him in person exactly three times, four including today."

"God, that sucks! I'd go crazy." She glanced over her shoulder at the nurses' station to make sure she wasn't needed. "Does it bother you when girls like me get all giggly around him?"

I shrugged again. "No, not really. I mean, he's hot, you can't deny it. I get it. I just happened to be lucky enough that he fell in love with me. What drives me nuts is the groupies that follow his band around on tour and try to seduce him even knowing he's got a wife."

The nurse's eyes boggled out. "They do that? For real? I mean, yeah, he's hot, and it's fun to imagine—I mean, um—yeah. He's hot, but I'd never *do* anything."

I laughed. "You're funny. The sad thing is, there are girls who'd do anything for a hot guy. It's kind of ridiculous. I mean, there are so many men out there, why do you have to be so deprived of morals that you'd seduce a married man?" I looked up at the little blonde nurse. "What's your name, by the way?"

"Andrea." She bit her lip and blushed scarlet when Chase came back in, carrying a styrofoam cup of coffee, another mini-can of Vernor's, and a cup of ice.

He smiled at Andrea as he handed me the ice. "I'm not sure I remember the last time I had coffee this burnt," he said, chuckling.

I glanced at Andrea, who was slowly edging away toward the door. "Andrea, this is my husband, Chase. Baby, this Andrea, one of our nurses."

Andrea shook his hand, her eyes wide. "Hi, Mr. Delany. I can make some new coffee for you, if you want. I'm not really a nurse yet. I'm an intern, so I'm really just here to observe and to help, but I'll do whatever you need, so if something comes up, just—" She cut herself off as if realizing she was rambling. "Anyway. I'll just—I'll go. Nice to meet you, both of you." She scurried out of the room and vanished before Chase could get a word in edgewise.

He laughed, giving me a puzzled look. "Well… that was odd. She didn't even give me time to see if she wanted an autograph."

I shook my head, shoulders shaking in silent laughter. "She was starstruck, baby. We were just talking about you, too, so she was probably kind of embarrassed."

Chase frowned, then shrugged. "Oh. She ran off like she was afraid of me or something."

"You are intimidatingly sexy, babe." I said, crunching on a piece of ice. I glanced at the group of nurses behind the desk, the number of whom seemed to have grown. "Maybe you should go out there and take some pictures with them or something."

Chase pinched the bridge of his nose. "I'm not here to take pictures with the nurses, Jay. You're about to have a baby. I'm here for you. For us."

"I know that. But they'll just keep clustering there and staring at us. Maybe if you take a few pictures and sign a few autographs, they'll be more likely to leave us alone." I sipped the soda and then tugged Chase closer by his hand. "Plus, it's hot watching you be all celebrity."

Chase winced as he swallowed a mouthful of coffee, which to my nose did smell incredibly burnt. "Yeah, I guess."

He set his coffee down and moved to stand in the doorway, waving over one of the nurses. He said something to her, too low for me to catch, then smiled at her, the brilliant, brain-melting smile that I realized was his professional smile, one that didn't quite reach his eyes. I watched the shift in him, the straightening of his posture, the eyes darting everywhere as the room filled with women of varying ages in scrubs of all colors. I watched in amusement as he worked the room with ease, spending a few minutes with each person, completely attuned and focused on the person he was talking to. He took individual pictures, then a couple with the group as a whole. He signed cell phone cases, scrub sleeves, receipts, a $20 bill, the inside of a romance novel cover, and the back of an e-reader.

His smile never faltered, and even in the midst of it all, he glanced at me frequently, a question in his eyes. I knew he'd clear the room out in an instant if I asked him to.

Eventually, the nurses left Chase slumped down into a chair. "God, that's exhausting," he said.

"Is it?" I said, genuinely interested. "It seems like it would be fun."

"It is fun, but it's tiring. Each person wants to feel special, wants your attention on them, but you can't ignore everyone else. So you have to be focused on whoever you're talking to, but still be aware of the people waiting. I've had people show up to more than one show and wait in line to meet me several times, and they always hope I'll remember them from show to show. And it's like, I try, but I meet hundreds of people at the post-show signings, and I just can't remember them all." Chase waved his hand, dismissing it. He leaned closer to me and touched my belly beneath the monitor lead. "How are you doing?"

I shrugged. "I want to have this baby. I've been here for, like, six hours already."

"How much longer do you think it'll take?" Chase asked.

"I have no idea," I said. "It could be hours still. I remember my mom saying she was in labor for, like, two days with me."

"God, I hope it doesn't take that long," Chase said.

"Me, too, believe me." I shifted in the bed, watching the monitor as another contraction clenched my uterus. "Even with the epidural, this is uncomfortable at best."

Three hours passed, with Chase slugging cup after cup of burnt coffee.

Five hours after Chase's arrival, Dr. Clayton appeared, checked my progress, and then washed his hands. "Good news and bad news. Good news is, you're almost completely effaced. Ninety percent or so, I'd say. Bad news is, you're only dilated to seven, so you haven't moved very much there. I'm going to turn up the pitocin a touch and see if that breaks things loose. If that doesn't help you along, I might think about breaking your water, but I don't necessarily want to do that just yet." He touched a button on the IV box and then turned to leave.

I nodded. "Okay." When he was gone, I addressed Chase. "All that just means I'm not ready yet, so we wait some more."

"Yay, more waiting!" Chase said with fake enthusiasm, laughing at the end to make it a joke. He sobered and asked, "Why wouldn't he want to break your water yet?"

I thought. "It makes you progress even faster, which can make you have the baby pretty much immediately. But there's only a short window of time to have the baby after breaking the water. If it takes too long, you have to have a C-section."

Seven in the morning brought a new on-call OB, a delicate Lebanese woman wearing a hijab. She said I had dilated to a nine and that my primary OB, Dr. Rayburn, was supposed to be at the hospital in an hour or two to decide whether to break my water or not. Chase had dark circles under his eyes, and I'd heard his stomach growling.

"Chase, you should go get something to eat. Nothing's going to happen until Dr. Rayburn gets here."

He shook his head. "I'm fine, baby. I'm not leaving."

I narrowed my eyes at him. "Go, Chase. Get some food. There's a cafeteria in the hospital. Just get a sandwich or something. You need to eat. Just because I can't doesn't mean you can't."

"Are you sure?"

I flapped my hands at him, since I couldn't actually get up to push him out the door. "The sound of your stomach growling is making me crazy. Go eat."

He hadn't been gone five minutes when I felt something wet spreading beneath my butt and up my back. I sat up and pushed the sheet away, touching the bed between my legs.

"Of course my water would break now." I touched the call button and then reached for my phone to text Chase to come back immediately. The message sent, and the "delivered" notice popped up.

A chime from the chair where Chase had been sitting brought another curse from me. He'd forgotten his phone.

A nurse came in, and that sparked a flurry of activity. The on-call showed up, put on one glove, and checked me.

"Oh, yes, it is time, Mrs. Delany. I can touch her head with my finger." The on-call's pager went off at that moment, and she stripped off the glove as she checked it. "Dr. Rayburn is here to deliver you. Just in time, it would seem."

"My husband is in the cafeteria and doesn't have his phone with him," I said. "Can someone find him for me?"

One of the nurses left at a run, and that was when I realized this wasn't just happening *soon*, it was happening *now*. The other nurses were moving around the room with quick efficiency, one shutting off the epidural and pitocin drips, transforming the room in readiness for the delivery.

Dr. Rayburn showed up, gloved, masked, and aproned, smiling calmly at me. "Ready, Jamie? You're about to be a mommy!"

"No! I'm not ready! Chase isn't here!" I felt panic hit me, along with the return of the agonizing contraction pain. I couldn't have this baby without Chase. He had to be here. He had to be.

Dr. Rayburn just nodded and waited to one side as the hospital bed was turned into a delivery chair, stirrups holding my legs apart. "Well, this baby is coming. I know Nina went to go find him. He'll be here, Jamie, but this is happening now. Okay? Just breathe for me, and don't push until I tell you."

Suddenly the instruction to breathe didn't seem so ridiculous. The pain was excruciating, so bitterly intense that each contraction, one after another in wave upon relentless wave, took my breath away. I had to clench my teeth and squeeze a breath past the weight of pain, suck in air, and try to breathe again along with the screams that ripped from my throat.

"Where the *fuck* is Chase? I need him!" I gritted out the words, curling over my belly and moaning in relief as the contraction passed, giving me a brief respite before another hit me.

"He's coming, Jamie. Breathe." Dr. Rayburn was there between my knees now. "Good. Now push, okay? Push hard, and when Laura gets to ten, stop pushing, okay? Ready? Now…push!"

I pushed, bearing down with every muscle in my body, holding my breath. The nurse next to me counted slowly—*one…two…three…four*—and I bore down, accompanying each counted number with a mental plea for Chase to come.

Chase…Chase…Chase…I need you…

I pushed and pushed, and when Laura said "Ten," I exhaled and went limp, out of breath and dizzy.

I felt him before I saw him. He slid into the room at a dead run, slamming into the doorpost and bouncing off, then taking his place at my side. I scrabbled for his hand, fixing my eyes on his as the next contraction hit me and Dr. Rayburn yelled for me to push, push, push, and I was screaming, not breathing, pushing, feeling something hard and hot and huge splitting me in two, shredding me from the inside out, agony so intense it was unreal, all-consuming, burning through me like fire. I heard Chase counting now instead of the nurse, and his voice was my only lifeline to reality, the only thing connecting me to anything but pain and pushing. I had Chase's hands in mine, and I felt him squeeze and heard him say "ten," but barely had time for a single deep breath when Dr. Rayburn was encouraging me to push still, push.

"She's crowning!" Dr. Rayburn was calm but enthusiastic. "You're doing great, Jamie! Keep pushing!"

Pure agony, raw and unadulterated, ripped through me, and I pushed with it, an enormous pressure within threatening to buckle my sanity, and still I pushed, sobbed in a breath and clutched Chase's hands with all my strength.

I heard screaming, knew it was me.

Chase's voice, counting slowly and rhythmically, pausing between ten and one to tell me he loved her, tell me I was doing great, she was almost there, telling me he saw Samantha, saw her head and some of one shoulder, I was almost done...

Another wave of soul-searing pain and screaming and breathless agony and dizziness from pushing, stars dancing in my vision, dots of white against wavering black as oxygen rushed into my starved lungs.

Heat, pressure, pain.

Push.

One...two...three...four...you're doing great, Jay, almost there, I see her arms...yes! Push again, one more time, baby...one...two...three...four...

Other voices, more pain, a feeling of ripping flesh and rippling contractions and Chase's counting voice cutting off between five and six, stuttering, laughing, saying my name.

And then, between one breath and another, between one heartbeat and another, it all stopped. I felt something slide and give way, felt the weight and pressure vanish, and Chase was kissing my cheek and whispering unintelligible words of love and encouragement.

"She's here!" Dr. Rayburn tugged, and I felt something slick leave my body. "Here she is! She's beautiful!"

I was dizzy and weak and couldn't breathe, but I listened.

Nothing.

Nothing.

"Why isn't she crying?" I heard my own voice from far away. "Dr. Rayburn? Why isn't Samantha crying?"

There was no answer, and I knew fear like no other.

"Samantha? Chase? What's going on?" Tears in my eyes, and clogging my voice.

I looked up at Chase, saw terror on his features. He was watching Dr. Rayburn, clutching my hand so hard it was going numb.

"Got it...thank god," Dr. Rayburn's voice, pitched low, more to herself than out loud but falling into a space of silence.

I couldn't see anything but Chase, and I saw relief flood his eyes. I heard a *smack*, and then the most welcome sound I'd ever heard.

The indignant squalling of a newborn.

I breathed, really breathed, for the first time in what felt like days. As I sucked in cool air into my hot lungs, I felt a presence at my side and opened my eyes to see Dr. Rayburn cradling a blue paper-wrapped bundle.

I struggled upright, took the crinkling paper and tiny weight into my arms. A little pale pink fist waved in the air, and the cries filled my ears, washed over me. Little dark eyes met mine, and the cries stopped for a moment.

Mother gazed at daughter, and for a moment, the universe stopped.

Something within me shook, shuddered, broke open, and I was filled an inrushing flood of overwhelming love. I heard myself sob, took the tiny fist between two fingers, and brushed my daughter's face, her cheek, her scalp, touched her so-soft skin still crusted with blood and effluvia.

"Hi, Samantha." I kissed her nose and tried not to drip tears on her. "Samantha May Delany."

Chase's grandmother was Samantha's middle namesake, since Samantha was my grandmother's name.

Chase's face filled my vision, and I turned my face up to his, saw his eyes wet and tears streaming down his face, his eyes glazed with a welter of emotion. "You did it, Jay. *You* did it." His voice was barely audible.

I sobbed again and gestured to him with the bundle of baby. "Go see your daddy."

Chase leaned down and gingerly settled his daughter into the crook of his arm, the baby seeming even smaller against his huge frame and burly, tattooed arms.

"We did it," I whispered.

Chase just shook his head without taking his eyes off Samantha. "No, baby. You did it. God, you're amazing." He glanced at me, love and adoration in his eyes. "I love you so much, Jay."

I couldn't respond, too exhausted and amazed and overwhelmed to speak.

A nurse came and took Samantha from him, talking about tests. Chase came over to me and held my hands as the afterbirth was delivered, put his head next to mine and breathed with me as Dr. Rayburn did something painful to my bottom half.

After a few minutes, she stood up and stripped her delivery gear off. "You did amazing, Jamie." She washed her hands and stood next to me opposite Chase. "Four pounds, six ounces, eighteen inches. You want to go take some pictures, Daddy?"

I watched in bleary-eyed wonder as Chase took pictures with his phone, and I laughed when the nurse pressed Samantha's ink-black foot to his forearm, leaving a footprint on his skin. He took pictures of her after she was wrapped in a blue and white blanket, snuggled in my arms.

After the baby had been taken to be measured and tested, Dr. Rayburn came back. "Well, overall she looks pretty good, all things considered. She is a few weeks premature, so I'm worried about her breathing. She's not quite as pink as I'd like, and she seems to be taking some pretty shallow breaths. She might need some assistance for a while, so just be aware she might have to stay here for a while until her oxygen levels even out and she gains a little weight." She patted my leg. "You look great, though, Jamie. You tore a little, so I had to give you about seven or eight stitches, but nothing excessive. For now, you need to eat and get some rest."

And then we were alone once more. Chase sat on the edge of the bed and traced my face with a forefinger, and I in turn touched the miniature footprint on his forearm.

"I'm gonna get that tattooed on, right there," Chase said, touching the dried ink.

It would make an awesome tattoo. Maybe I'd get one to match.

A nurse brought a tray of food, which I devoured faster than I should have, probably. Exhaustion was washing over me then, tugging me under, drowning me. I'd been fighting it, knowing I needed to eat and wanting to see Samantha again before I slept, but it was futile. Chase stroked my hair and my back with a tender hand, his fingers eventually moving to thread into mine, and I let myself go, feeling complete and safe under his watchful gaze.

I fell asleep, and the last thought before descending into the drowsing depths of sleep was, *I'm a mommy.*

Chapter 7: Anna

I HEARD MY PHONE RINGING. It was distant, hazy. I struggled up through the fog of sleep, reaching for it even as I felt Jeff stir next to me, nudging me with his foot and mumbling, "Phone's ringing."

I snagged it off the nightstand and brought it to my ear. I'd forgotten it was plugged in, though, so the cord jerked it out of my hands to fall, still ringing, between the nightstand and the bed. I cursed floridly, reaching for it, unable to quite grasp it. Still swearing, I finally managed to grab it with my thumb and forefinger, swiping the "answer" tab immediately.

"Hello?" I sounded out of breath and frustrated. The clock on the nightstand read eight-oh-six in the morning.

"Uh, hi, Anna. It's Chase." He sounded exhausted and exhilarated.

"Hi, Chase. How's Jamie?" I felt Jeff sit up next to me.

"She had the baby about an hour ago."

"An hour ago?" I shrieked. "She was supposed to call me first so I could be there! God, we're so fighting!"

Chase laughed. "I'll tell her you said that. Things happened really suddenly, though. We were in a holding pattern for a long time, just waiting. Then her water broke and she had the baby within, like, fifteen minutes."

"Gotcha. We'll be there in a few minutes. Congrats, Chase! You're a daddy! How does it feel?"

"It's amazing. It was, no lie, the most incredible experience of my entire life." I heard him sigh, holding the phone away from his mouth. "She's actually sleeping right now, but they're going to move us to a recovery room soon. Well, soon in hospital terms."

"So, like, four hours?" I said.

"Exactly. Have some breakfast before you come up. There's no rush. We'll be here."

"Okay. What room are you in?" I asked.

"I'll text you the room number when we get moved."

"Okay." I paused. "Chase? I'm happy for you. You'll be a great daddy."

"Thanks, Anna." He hung up, and I flopped back on the bed.

"She had the baby an hour ago," I said.

"Well, let's get our asses up and showered, have some breakfast, and go see them." Jeff suited action to words, moving into the bathroom and starting the shower.

Instead of getting in himself, though, he returned to the bed and dragged me out, pushing me to the bathroom, stripping me of my nightshirt and panties in the process. I had been laughing up until he pushed my panties off and knelt in front of me on the bathroom tile, a hungry look on his face. I leaned back against the sink, staring down at Jeff's blazing brown eyes. He ran his hands up from my ankles to my knees, up the backs of my thighs, carving hot trails around between them in a teasing brush along my folds.

My breath caught, and I closed my eyes in anticipation. I felt his fingers close around my ankle and lift. I cooperated, setting my foot on the closed lid of the toilet, holding the edge of the sink with both hands for balance. His fingers slid up the inside of my thigh, sliced through my folds, and swiped through the slick heat deep inside me. I gasped and felt my knees weaken, then buckle when his tongue slid against my clit and began slow circles around it. I let go of the sink with one hand to run my fingers through his soft, brown, close-cropped hair, pulling him against me as the fire began to boil in my core. Two fingers slipped inside me and curled against my G-spot, buckling my knees again and sending lances of lightning through me.

I felt myself riding the edge, teetering on the brink of climax. Instead of letting him bring me over the edge, I tugged him up, tilting his face away from my core. "I need you. I want you inside me. I want us to come together."

He stood up slowly, and I felt the tip of his cock nudge against me. I wrapped my leg around his hip, and he held it there, lifting up on his toes to enter me. As he slid into me, he leaned in to kiss me, his tongue spearing into my mouth. My belly was in the way, though, so he had to lean back to thrust into me. I still had one hand gripping the sink for balance, and I put my other hand on his shoulder, pulling myself up and sliding down to meet his thrust. He leaned away from me, stretching his cock as far as it would comfortably go, and we both watched as he drew out and slid back in, setting a slow rhythm. I watched my folds stretch around him, watched his thick length driving in and sliding out, finding something erotic in the play of skin against skin, against the wet glistening of his cock and the way we fit together so perfectly.

Jeff's free hand slipped between our bodies to touch the hypersensitive nub of my clit, barely touching it, brushing it with a feather-light caress that had me jerking and arching my back, needing more, wanting all he could give me.

The only sound was our bodies meeting, wet sliding, slick sucking, mouths kissing and breath gasping, fingers scratching and scraping. Then the heat billowed through me and stirred me hotter, and Jeff's strokes grew frantic and his fingers on my clit circled rough and pushed against me and made me wild and touched me so perfectly. He lifted up on his toes and jerked me closer by the leg, fingers clutching my thigh and pulling me behind the knee, and each thrust of his cock had me gasping, sent my body to trembling and spasming and gasping. My head lolled back on my shoulders and I felt my breasts bouncing with each thrust, and I knew he was still holding himself back, still forcing himself into a measure of gentility, and I loved him all the more for it.

I careened over the edge into climax without warning, digging my fingers into his bicep and whispering his name in a breathless prayer. I felt him release in that moment, at the exact instant of my orgasm. I knew he'd been keeping it back, holding, waiting until I came. God, the man always, *always* knew how to give me exactly what I needed.

Is it bad that one of the things I loved most about my relationship with Jeff was our sex life? I mean, don't get me wrong, that's the only thing, and it's not the thing I love the most about Jeff as a man, but our sexual relationship never failed to leave me breathless. Even when it was plain old vanilla missionary in the dark on a Sunday night, it was perfect. He was perfect. Slow and sweet when I needed him tender, rough and ready fucking when I needed him powerful and erotic.

And this? Standing up in the bathroom, thirty-four weeks pregnant? God, so amazing.

If you'd told me yesterday that I'd be fucking Jeff like this, I'd have laughed at you. I'd have told you there was no way I could manage standing sex at this stage of my pregnancy. Yet here I was, coming so hard I could barely breathe, clutching Jeff for dear life as my entire body convulsed, my leg slipping from his grip and driving him deeper inside me, his cock still spasming and thrusting, our mouths crashing together in a rough and raw kiss of desperate love, furious expression of need.

We breathed together for long minutes as we regained our bearings.

And then the contractions struck. The first one hit me like a ton of bricks, my womb clamping down with enough force to leave me doubled over, gasping for breath.

"Anna? Shit, Anna?"

I pulled myself upright, clinging to Jeff with both hands as another contraction hit me hard on heels of the first. "It should pass," I gasped. "Sex can cause contractions, but it rarely induces labor. Just...just give me a minute."

I felt Jeff's worried gaze on me, and but I ignored it, resting my cheek on his chest and breathing through the pain. Finally the contraction left me, and I was able to straighten and stand on my own.

"See?" I said, "It's gone."

"Maybe we shouldn't—" Jeff started.

"Oh, hell no," I interrupted. "Unless the doctor tells us we can't, you're not taking away my orgasms. Especially since I'll be without them for six weeks after the birth. I read on some Internet mommy's chat-board that these contractions are actually good somehow. They soften the cervix or something."

Jeff frowned. "It looked painful."

I shrugged. "It was. It's worth it to me, though." I pushed him toward the shower, which was still running. "Now get in before we don't have any hot water left."

I was getting worried. I hadn't said anything to Jeff, but the contractions hadn't actually stopped completely. I'd read that they could last on and off all day after sex, but that they should be irregular. Mine were spaced about ten minutes apart like clockwork, and they had been all throughout the shower, breakfast, and the drive to the hospital. I managed to keep my reactions down to a wince every now and again. Jeff noticed, I think, but didn't say anything.

Jamie was awake by the time we got to the hospital around ten-thirty. She was eating and talking with Chase when we entered the room, looking alert, although both she and Chase wore rather subdued expressions. I hugged Jamie, sitting on the edge of her bed.

"Hey, hooker. How are you feeling?"

"Like I just shit a bowling ball," she joked. "Actually, I feel okay. Tender, tired, and happy."

I examined her closely, and the tension lines around her mouth and eyes didn't escape me. "What aren't you telling me?"

She shrugged. "Samantha is a preemie, Anna. There's complications. She's having trouble breathing on her own. She's at risk for RSV. I haven't even seen or held her since she came out, except for literally a minute when I first had her." Jamie sniffed, and I could tell she was barely holding herself together, which made sense of the angst I could feel radiating off Chase from across the room.

"Why don't you give us a minute, guys," I said.

"I'm not gonna—" Chase began.

"I'm fine, Chase. Just go. Give me a minute with Anna." The guys both left, reluctantly, and

Jamie threw her arms around me. "I'm scared for her, Anna. I mean, she's not in critical condition or anything, but I'm just...I just hate this."

"She'll be okay, Jay. You know she will. She'll be out of here and home with you and Chase before you know it." I held her tight. "I'm proud of you, Mama."

Jamie sniffled again and then pushed me away playfully. "What about you? When are you getting induced?"

"Supposed to be next week." I touched my belly as another contraction rippled through me, right on time, ten minutes from the last one.

Jamie didn't miss my reaction. "But it might be sooner, huh?"

I grimaced as the contraction blistered through me. When it passed, I shrugged, shaking my head. "I don't know. Jeff and I had sex this morning, and it started these contractions. They're supposedly normal, and they're supposed to go away eventually."

"But?"

"They haven't gone away. They're coming every ten minutes, and they're freaking *strong*."

"Have you told Jeff?" Jamie asked.

"Not yet. I don't want to worry him unless I have to. I keep hoping they'll go away. I've been moving around, walking, all that." I stood up and walked the few steps across the room and back.

"I think you probably should ask someone about it. What if you're in labor? I mean, you don't want the babies to just fall out, you know?"

I snorted, sitting down on the bed next to Jamie again, giving her shoulder a playful shove. "You're such an idiot, Jay."

"Yeah, but you love me." She rubbed my belly. "You really should get checked out, though."

Jeff, Chase, and a nurse pushing a mobile bassinet entered the room. The nurse brought the cart with the clear plastic cradle to a stop at the foot of the bed and lifted up a tiny bundle wrapped in the blue and white hospital swaddling blanket. She settled the baby into Jamie's arms and stepped away.

"She's been doing a lot better for the last few hours," the nurse said. "Her O-two levels have been pretty stable on her own, so Dr. Mansour thought you might like to spend some time with her."

The transformation that came over Jamie was immediate, and shocking. She cradled her daughter against her chest, a blissful smile on her lips, her eyes wide and shining and happier than I'd ever seen her. "Oh, my god, hi," Jamie said, her voice pitched high in that tone of voice we instinctively use with babies. "Hi there, beautiful. Look at you, oh, you're awake. And you look just like Daddy, such dark hair and beautiful brown eyes."

Chase circled to the other side of the bed and stared down at his wife and daughter.

Surreptitiously, I watched Chase as he gazed at his family. I may not have been in love with him, but I still cared for him, and to see him so happy made me happy.

I turned to look at Jeff, who was watching the whole thing with an expression of rapt interest. *This is going to be us soon*, his expression said.

At that moment, of course, another contraction hit me, harder than ever and less than ten minutes since the previous one. I couldn't stop a hiss from escaping, my hand covering my belly, the other braced on the bed. Before, they'd only lasted maybe twenty or thirty seconds total, but this one had me in its grip for nearly a minute.

"Anna? I thought they'd stopped?" Jeff, from beside me, hand on my back, voice a complex mix of concerned and irritated.

I blew out a long breath between pursed lips as the contraction finally passed. "Well, they didn't," I said, irritable from the pain. "I thought they would. They're getting stronger and closer together."

Jeff growled. "Damn it, Anna. You should have told me *hours* ago."

"I didn't want to worry you if it was nothing."

Jeff tugged me to my feet. "Well, now I'm worried and irritated at the same time, which is just super awesome." He pulled me out into the hall, pressed my back against the wall beside the door, and cupped my face in his hands, forcing my gaze to his. "Anna. You're *supposed* to worry me with this shit. It's my job. Letting me love you means letting me worry about every little thing."

"Jeff, I—" I tried to look away, but he wouldn't let me, so I brought my eyes back to his. "I'm sorry. I should have told you."

"Damn right." He touched my lips with his, a caress more than a kiss. "Now, let's go find a doctor for you and see if you're in labor."

I was in labor.

Eighty percent effaced and dilated to a seven.

My doctor was pissed.

Then came the bad news: Caleb was in a breech position, and if he didn't turn, they'd have to do a C-section.

Bridge

JEFF PACED THE HALLWAY, trying to get his breathing under control. The helplessness was a fiery rage in his blood, a dark and angry force shuddering in his blood, his brain. His hands shook, his heart hammered, stuttered, machine-gun pattered.

She was in pain, contractions ripping through her in relentless waves, pain turning her lovely features into a rictus of agony. Sweat dampened her hair, fine strands sticking to her forehead, lines etched into her brow, mouth set, full lips pressed flat. Fingers clutching the bed rail so hard her knuckles turned white.

And Jeff could do nothing. Nothing.

They were only giving her another hour before they did an emergency C-section. Before they cut her open and pulled the babies out. He knew it was normal, but the idea of C-section still freaked him the hell out.

Jeff found himself at the end of the hallway, fists clenched, head pressed against the cold wall. He felt a hand on his shoulder and turned around.

"Hey, man. You all right?" It was Chase, of all people.

"Do I look okay?" Jeff knew he was being a dick, but he couldn't help it.

He'd learned to get along with Chase to an extent, but he'd never be best friends with him.

Chase withdrew his hand and stood a few feet away from Jeff, spinning his cell phone between a thumb and forefinger. "I know you and I aren't, like, best buddies or whatever, Jeff, but...look, I know it's hard, okay? It sucks, not being able to do anything." He shoved his phone in his pocket and moved to stand in front of Jeff. "It's going to be okay. Anna's tough. You and I both know that."

"She's in pain, and there's nothing I can do. It fucking sucks. I need to do something, help her, I don't know. Not just stand there and hope for the best."

"I know. How do you think I felt when I found out Jamie was getting induced and I was in fucking Chicago? What if something had happened and I wasn't there? But you gotta know they know what they're doing. They'll take care of her. She'll be fine. Just be there with her. Be there for her." Chase clapped Jeff on the shoulder. "Like I said, I know we're not necessarily friends, Jeff, but I do still care about Anna, in that I want to see her happy and healthy. You make her happy, and I can see you're a good man. If you need a friend, you've got one." Chase turned away then, leaving Jeff stunned.

He stood watching as Chase slowly walked away, only finding his voice after several heartbeats. "Chase?" he called out, and the other man stopped, turned around. "Thanks. And congratulations. Samantha is beautiful."

Back in the room with Anna, Jeff found her in the same basic position, clutching the railings, sweating, grimacing through the pain. He sat beside her, soul wrung dry, hands trembling with raw emotion. When the contraction subsided, all he could do was whisper love to her, hold her limp hand, and wait some more.

Each time a contraction ripped through her, she tried to tough it out in silence but couldn't, and long, groaning, soul-searing screams of pain were drawn from deep within her. Each scream, each moan, each gasp shredded Jeff. Then she went limp when the contraction passed, and her eyes turned to him, fixed on him with such complete adoration that he wanted to weep.

An hour passed, taffy-stretched slow in some moments, and rocket-ship fast in others.

A technician moved an ultrasound wand over Anna's belly, and even Jeff could see the truth: Caleb was still breech.

Chapter 8: Anna

I DIDN'T WANT TO SCREAM ANYMORE. I wanted to be that tough kind of woman who endures the pain of childbirth in silence; my throat ached, scraped raw, because I wasn't that kind of woman. I sucked in long breaths, eyes closed and knees drawn up, fingers clutching the bed railing so hard I didn't think I could let go on my own.

I felt Jeff next to me, and I knew he felt helpless. I wanted to tell him it was okay, it would be worth it all when we held our little babies. Words wouldn't come out, though, stolen as another wave of excruciation sliced through me.

I heard voices, felt something wet and cold on my belly, then a hard probing and sliding across my skin: an ultrasound. I tried to pry my eyes open to see the screen, but my sight was blurred and wavering.

"He's still breech," a voice said. "We'll have to do an emergency C-section."

I wanted to cry, but I also knew it would mean an end to the pain.

I saw ceiling tiles overhead, moving. Long breaths in and out, wrenching pain, more voices, fluorescent lights, doors opening, Jeff telling me to breathe, *it's okay, baby, just breathe for me*, in and out, breathe in and one, two three, more pain, things happening to my body, motion, blue papery fabric wrapped over me. Things happened around me, and then the massive clenching pressure of contractions stopped and I could breathe. The absence of pain was so blessed, so incredible that I was woozy, dizzy, disoriented with relief. I felt Jeff's hand in mine. I forced my eyes open, relieved all over again that the pain had stopped, and I knew I should know why, but didn't.

"Hi." It was all I could manage.

"Hi, baby. We're in the OR." Jeff's voice was tender and quiet.

"I can't feel my toes." I tried to wiggle them; nothing. "What happened to my toes?"

"Anesthetic, Anna." Jeff's fingers squeezed mine. His strength and warmth was reassuring.

"So I still have my toes?" It seemed important, but I wasn't sure why. I felt foggy and delirious.

"Yes, honey. You still have your toes." Jeff was laughing, and I saw his face above me, smiling at me.

I sucked in deep breaths, blew them out, and gradually clarity returned. "They're doing the C-section?"

Jeff nodded. "There you are. Back with me now?" He brushed strands of sweat-damp hair away from my face. "Yeah. Caleb is still breech, and they can't wait any longer."

A wall of blue blocked my sight of my body from the waist down, but Jeff was by my head, dressed in scrubs, with worry etched on his rugged features. I felt pressure on my belly, tugging. Voices issuing calm instructions floated to me from the other side of the partition. I was glad I couldn't see what was going on. Out of the corner of my eye I saw a nurse turn away from my body, and her gloved hands were coated in blood. I had to look away, focused on Jeff's jawline, hard and strong and rough with days' worth of beard. It kind of suited him, actually.

"I don't think I tell you enough how handsome you are, Jeff." I was filled with fear and excitement and panic and worry, and it seemed like an important thing to tell him.

He looked down at me, carving a caressing line down my cheekbone with his thumb. "You're amazing, Anna. I love you so much. You're doing great. They've almost got the first baby out."

I felt a strange pulling sensation, and then I heard a sound that would forever be imprinted on my soul: the shuddering breath and stuttering cry of a wailing infant. Jeff's face contorted as he watched over the top of the curtain, and I could read the play of emotions across his face: awe, amazement, wonder, love, shock.

"It's Niall, honey. They have Niall. God, she's beautiful, she's perfect. Just like you." His voice caught, and he blinked hard several times.

A few heartbeats passed, and then a female voice spoke up. "Dad? You want to cut the rest of the cord?"

I turned my head to the side. A warmer sat a few feet away, this side of the curtain and away from the sterile surgical area. Niall lay on the warmer, mostly cleaned up and kicking and wailing, waving tiny fists. A nurse had a length of purplish-red umbilical cord clamped off and held it out to Jeff, while another handed him a pair of odd-looking scissors. Jeff turned to look back at me, and I smiled my encouragement at him, barely recognizing the activity still happening to the rest of me. He slid the scissors between the clamps and cut the cord, and then Niall was wrapped in a blanket and handed to Jeff.

Just as I'll never forget the first time I heard Niall's crying voice, I'll never forget that image: Jeff, huge arms flexing in the sleeves of his scrub shirt as he reached for his daughter, a tiny, wailing bundle of swaddling blanket and waving fists fitting snugly into the crook of his arms. His face, so handsome, turning soft and tender and awestruck. The feather-light kiss of his lips to her forehead, the barely contained emotions warring on his features. His eyes smiling at me, looking at me with such love that my heart couldn't contain it all.

The strange tugging sensation came again, and then I heard Caleb's voice cry his displeasure.

Jeff was next to me again, and this time he couldn't hold it back. A tear slipped down his cheek, and he bent over me, kissed my forehead, then my lips. "Anna, god, Anna. Caleb is here. Caleb is out. He's so amazing." He looked down at me, his deep brown eyes soft with emotion, wet with tears. "I love you so much. You did it. God, Anna. I'm so proud of you."

The cord-cutting ritual happened again, and then Caleb was hurried away, all too soon. I barely got a glimpse of him, and then he was gone.

"Will I get to hold them soon?" It was all I could think of. I reached for Jeff, now cradled in Jeff's arms, only to discover that my arms were strapped to the table.

A young male face, acne-scarred, hair contained in the stupid-looking sterile hat, a mask around his mouth, appeared from behind the curtain. "You'll get to hold them soon, Mrs. Cartwright. You have to get stitched up first, okay? As soon as you're able, we'll bring your babies to you."

"Can I at least kiss Caleb?" I had to touch one of my babies at the very least. I had to know it was all real, that this was happening, that it wasn't a dream, that my babies were healthy.

The nurse nodded his approval and Jeff brought Caleb over to me, crouched down and put Caleb's forehead to my lips. When my lips touched his skin, when I saw his thick thatch of dark wet hair, I lost it. Tears streamed down my face, and I couldn't wipe them away.

Another nurse took Caleb from Jeff and set him in the warmer, recording his weight, stretched him out and marked his height at head and foot on the paper liner with a pen, and then Caleb was gone and Jeff was next to me, wiping my face with gentle fingers.

The next few hours passed with startling swiftness. I was wheeled out of the OR, unstrapped—to my great relief—and brought to a recovery room. I was shaking uncontrollably, my hands trembling so badly Jeff had to hold the straw in a can of soda to my lips, because when I tried to pick up the can on my own, I shook it so bad it sloshed over my hand. I ached so badly. The anesthetic was wearing off, and my entire lower half was a knotted mass of pins and needles, as if my legs had fallen asleep. The pins and needles got so bad that I wanted to scream. It felt like a thousand bees were buzzing under my skin, crawling and stinging. I rubbed my thighs almost frantically, trying to erase the sensation, but it didn't work. Eventually, Jeff took one of my legs and settled it across his lap and began massaging the muscles, starting at my thigh and working his way down to my calf and then my foot, moving to the other leg and repeating the process.

It was the best massage I'd ever gotten.

An older, silver-haired woman in the colorful pattern-printed scrubs of an NICU nurse entered the recovery room, followed by two other women in plain dark blue scrubs.

"Ready to meet your babies?" the NICU nurse asked.

"God, yes. How are they doing?" I tried to stand up, but didn't even manage to rock forward to a fully sitting position.

"Why don't you let us help you into a wheelchair, and we'll take to them so you can find out for yourself?" The nurse, whose name tag announced her name as Sheila, helped me get my feet under me.

I was helped into a wheelchair, and they pushed me down endless corridors and around corners and through open doorways to the NICU ward. It was a wide room with rows of incubators and warmers, smelling of baby and milk and hospital. Machines buzzed quietly and efficiently, a baby fussed hungrily in one of the warmers, and in one corner a nurse cradled a baby in her arms, teasing the baby's lips with a bottle of formula.

Jeff walked beside me as I was wheeled to a stop between side-by-side incubators. I looked from one baby to the other, drinking in their features, seeing my nose, Jeff's eyes, a mixup of both of us. I couldn't tell them apart. I didn't know which was which. Shouldn't I be able tell? Guilt hit me. These were my babies, and I didn't know which was which? Did that mean I was a bad mommy? I had to hold back tears.

"Which one is which?" I asked, my voice quavering.

Sheila smiled at me, understanding pouring from her in nearly visible waves. "It's perfectly normal to not be able to tell them apart yet, hon." She reached into one of the incubators and carefully lifted the swaddled bundle out, settling it in my arms.

It? Had I just thought of my baby as an it? Another shudder ran through me.

"This is your daughter," Sheila said, fussing with the little cotton cap on Niall's head, tugging it farther down around her ears.

Niall was awake and quiet, brown eyes wide, searching, roving, and then...she fixed her eyes on me, focusing. A hot rush of emotion hit me, a Niagara flood of love and overwhelming protective need and awe and wonder. I'd made this warm thing in my arms, this little human, this tiny person. She was mine. Mine and Jeff's. I looked up at him, smiled at him, felt his love wash over me.

Sheila smiled at us, patted me on the back. "Dad, you can hold Caleb if you want, then you can trade. They're doing very well, both of them. They have mild jaundice, but that's normal for any baby, premature twins especially. They're breathing fairly well, although they'll need some help now and again. We'll have to see how they eat, though."

"How big are they?" I asked.

"Niall is three pounds, nine ounces, seventeen point three inches," Sheila answered. "Caleb is three pounds, four ounces, and sixteen point eight inches. They've both taken a bottle, but Caleb had a bit of trouble latching on. His sister didn't have any trouble, though. She latched on right away and sucked the bottle down like a champ."

I looked at Caleb, nestled in Jeff's powerful arms. "Let's switch," I said. "I want to hold him now."

Jeff slipped his hand under Niall in my arms, lifted her free, and for a moment had both of his babies in his arms. His smile in that moment was one of absolute joy. I saw his phone denting the breast pocket of his scrubs, so I reached up and grabbed it out of the pocket, pulled up the camera function, and took several pictures of my husband holding both of his children. He settled them both in my arms, and I felt the same look of contentment wash over me. I saw Jeff snapping pictures out of the corner of my eye, but I had eyes only for my babies. Niall, on the left, drowsing now, eyes closing, hands lax against her chin, Caleb on the right, fussing noisily, mouth working open and closed, hands waving and little fingers flexing.

Such tiny fingers. Everything about them was just...so small. So fragile. So perfect.

Jeff took Niall from me, and then Sheila brought me a bottle. I held it to Caleb's lips, and he nuzzled it with his mouth but didn't take it. He cried louder, his mews of hunger turning to wails of anger. A drop of formula touched his tongue, and he wailed even harder but refused to take the nipple of the bottle. Sheila showed me how to encourage him to take it, teasing his upper lip with the dripping tip. After several tries, he latched on and began sucking, his cries silencing.

"Will I be able to breastfeed them?" I asked.

Sheila stood back, watching him drink. "Yes, of course. For now we need to be able to monitor how much they're eating, though, so we'll have to continue to bottle-feed them. They both have to be at least four pounds, eight ounces, and able to drink an entire bottle at every feeding before they go home. We might have you try to breastfeed them the next time they're hungry, just to see how they latch on."

"How long will they be here, do you think?" Jeff asked.

Sheila shrugged. "It depends, really. A few days at least, maybe a week or two."

It wouldn't end up working out quite that easily, though. I didn't know that then, of course.

Chapter 9: Jamie

A WEEK AND HALF HAD PASSED since I'd had Samantha. She'd done well enough after birth that they'd sent her home, but now, as I held her in my arms, I worried. Her legs were mottled various shades of red and pink, splotches of color and paleness alternating like the patches of a jaguar. She seemed to be struggling to breathe, sucking in hard for each breath, lifting her chin to gasp for air. Her shirt was hiked up around her armpits, and I watched as her stomach dipped in with each breath, distending with each exhale, her diaphragm showing at the inhale.

Something was wrong.

Chase was out on the back porch of Kelly's house, where we were staying until we got the okay to drive home to New York. The sliding glass door

was open, and I could hear the start-and-stop guitar of Chase writing a song. I glanced back down
at Samantha, her sleeping face looking distressed.

Kelly sat down on the couch next to me. "How
are we doing, Mama?"

I looked at her, and I knew my worry was
stamped on my face. "She looks like she's having
trouble breathing."

Kelly took Samantha from me, resting the
baby face up on her legs. She pressed her thumb
into Samantha's skin, watching as the thumbprint
remained for several seconds before disappearing.
She pushed up Samantha's shirt a bit more and
watched her chest retract and expand with each
breath, tilting her watch upside down to time the
space between breaths.

Kelly turned to me with concern in her eyes.
"I think you need to take her to the E.R., Jamie. I
don't have an at-home pulse oximeter to measure
it, but I'm pretty sure Samantha's levels are low. It
could be RSV."

That was a word I'd heard tossed about before
they let us bring her home. I wasn't sure what it
was exactly, but I knew it had something to do
with her breathing. "Will she be okay?"

Kelly wouldn't quite meet my eyes. "You need
to take her to the hospital to get checked out,
sweetie."

I picked up Samantha and held her to my chest. "Get Chase, tell him what's going on. I'll get Sam in her car seat."

Within minutes, we were making the short trip back to Beaumont. Chase dropped Sam, Kelly, and me off at the emergency entrance and went to park the car. We were hustled to a triage room almost immediately, probably thanks to the fact that the nurses all knew Kelly. Chase joined us shortly thereafter, and then after more than thirty minutes, a young Indian man in a lab coat—looking too young to me to possibly be a doctor—checked over Samantha, almost cursorily.

"It is RSV, there is no doubt. She is not yet coughing or wheezing that I have seen, so it does not seem to be bronchiolitis as yet, but that is my worry. Her pulse-ox is seventy-four, which is very worrisomely low. It should be one hundred, or very close to it." He traced a fingernail along her diaphragm, which was visible at every inhale. "You can see here that she is having to work to take in breaths. I am going to admit her and have her taken up to the pediatric ward."

I struggled to keep my tears of panic at bay. "What can you do to help her?"

He gave me a serious, compassionate look. "Unfortunately, at her young age, there is nothing we can give her beyond saline and a little very diluted oxygen. She is too newly born to be given steroids or anything like that." His faint accent lilted at every other syllable. "We will monitor her, and we will do everything that we are able to keep your daughter healthy."

After an hour's wait, a nurse showed up to take us to the pediatric ward several floors up. My heart pounded, and I had to focus on deep breathing to keep from breaking down. Chase's hand in mine was a lifeline, warm and solid and comforting. It was all that kept me sane.

The room was tiny, barely ten feet wide and fifteen long, split in half by a thin curtain. Against either wall was a huge crib that could be converted into an incubator. A well-built male nurse in his thirties with sandy blond hair cropped short and a day's worth of stubble on his fair skin greeted us warmly. He introduced himself as Brian, and said he'd be our nurse until shift change in four hours. He spent several minutes with Samantha, checking her over himself, familiarizing himself with her chart, taking her temperature, listening to her breathing with a stethoscope, changing her from her own clothes to a hospital onesie that allowed him to attach monitor leads to her wrist and and a pulse-oximeter to her big toe.

That was what broke me: the sight of my baby, not even two weeks old, with a miniature cannula inserted into her nose and trailing over her shoulder, red and green wires with monitor leads taped to her wrist, an oximeter pinching her big toe, glowing red. I collapsed backward into a plasticky leather recliner, buried my face in my hands, and sobbed. Chase didn't try to comfort me beyond a heavy hand on my shoulder.

"I know it's scary to see her like this," Brian said, "but she's going to be okay. We're going to take great care of her, and you'll be home as soon as possible."

I nodded, barely hearing him. It didn't seem like it was going to be okay. Samantha lay in the crib, swaddled in a blanket with the lead wires trailing out near her shoulder, eyes narrowed but open. Her little mouth was partially open, and she was visibly struggling to draw in breath. I could only watch her, eyes burning with unshed tears, and try to breathe for her. I sucked in a breath as she did, let out mine with her, as if I could lend her my oxygen, as if I could heal her with sheer force of will.

Hours passed, streaming by like water, then stopping to creep by in a sludge-slow crawl. I sat in the chair, watching Samantha try to breathe, ignoring Chase's attempts to call me. At some point, Kelly left. Each labored breath in caused my heart to ache.

I was completely helpless.

I didn't notice him leave, but at some point, Chase shoved a styrofoam cup of khaki-colored coffee in my hands, too hot, burnt, too sweet, but exactly what I needed. The only sounds were Samantha's breathing, now laced with an occasional wheeze, and the incessant coughing of the baby on the other side of the curtain. When Sam coughed for the first time, I cried again.

There were no windows and no clocks, no way to measure the passage of time. It could have been midnight; it could have been noon. We'd left for the hospital around four in the afternoon, I thought, but wasn't sure. Chase was antsy, bouncing his knees, sitting in another chair drawn up near mine, continually running his hands through his hair. Then he began humming, mumbling, standing up and pacing the few steps down the length of the room and back, clearly caught up in something in his head. He left the room, and I heard him ask the nurses at the station for a pen and pencil, and then he returned and resumed his seat on the edge of the chair, scribbling on the pad of paper furiously.

I didn't disturb him, knowing he'd share it when he was ready.

Abruptly, he stopped pacing, facing me. "I'm supposed to be onstage in Lancaster, Pennsylvania, right now," he said.

I wasn't sure what his point was, so I just stared at him, not trusting myself to not completely lose my shit at him.

"I had this song for Samantha just pop in to my head. I need to get it out."

I just nodded, glanced at Samantha while chewing on my nail.

He took a breath, then started singing *a capella*. The melody was a lullaby, lilting and sweet and kind of haunting and quiet.

I can't breathe for you,
My darling,
I can't hold you close enough.
There's nothing I can do,
It doesn't matter if I'm strong or if I'm tough.
Because there's no way for me to imbue
Any of my strength into you.
I can only watch and pray,
I can only stand and stay
In this room close by your side,
Praying to a God I've long denied.
You're so tiny in that bed,
My darling,
You're so pale, and, god, so still.
And I can only watch and pray,
I can only stand and stay,
Wishing your body wasn't ill.
I can't breathe for you,
My darling,
There's just nothing I can do.
But I'm here, just the same,
Praying over you, I'm watching over you.
I can't ever hold you close enough,
My darling,

I can't ever be strong enough.
But I'll always, always try,
I'll comfort you when you cry.
I kiss away your tears,
I'll quiet all your fears.
I can't breathe for you,
My darling,
I can only watch and pray,
I can only stand stay
In this room, close to you.

By the end of the song, there was a crowd around the door, nurses, doctors, parents, orderlies. Chase's voice had never sounded so sweet or so soulful. He'd poured his heart into that song as fully as if he'd been on stage in front of thousands of people. When people realized the song was over, they seemed unsure what to do. Clapping seemed inappropriate to them in this setting, I think, but they knew a performance when they saw it. In the end, they scattered one by one, and Chase and I were left alone with our sick, sleeping daughter.

Chase swayed on his feet, stumbled, fell backward, and landed in the chair, scrubbing his face with his hands almost violently. When his shoulders began to shake, I realized he'd finally cracked the façade of his composure. I left my chair and knelt on the floor between his knees, still sore from childbirth but uncaring of my own discomfort in that moment. I pulled his face against my breast and held him, just held him. He only allowed himself a few moments of shuddering, silent tears before he breathed a harsh, gusting sigh and sat back, wiping his face.

"I don't know what came over me," he said, "I'm sorry—"

"Don't you dare apologize," I said, cutting in over him. "Our baby girl is sick, and there's nothing we can do but wait. You're allowed to be upset."

He nodded, rubbed his face again, breathing deeply. He pulled me onto his lap and I curled up into him, resting my head against his chest, listening to his heartbeat, watching the gentle rise and fall of Samantha's labored breathing.

At some point I dozed off, and was woken by a wet hacking cough coming from Samantha. Chase was asleep as well, head lolled back uncomfortably on the chair. I slid off his lap and stood over Samantha, taking her hand in mine. She curled her tiny fingers around my index finger and held on tight, cracking her eyes open to peer at me. Her face scrunched up and she coughed again, a wet, wracking cough that tore my heart to shreds.

A nurse came in, a different one now, a pretty woman in her thirties with blondes-streaked brown hair pulled into a bun. She introduced herself as Laurie and gently but firmly insinuated herself between me and Samantha, placing her stethoscope over Samantha's chest and listening as she coughed.

"I know this cough sounds really horrible," she said, turning to me, "but she doesn't have any crackles going on, and her pulse-ox is holding steady right around eighty. She's not ready to go home yet, but I don't think she's getting any worse. We'll keep the oxygen on for now, and if you notice a lot of drainage clogging her nose, you can clean it out." She showed us how to do that, squirting some saline into her nose and suctioning it out with a green bulb syringe.

Samantha absolutely hated this process, kicking and screaming and flailing, but she seemed to breathe easier after it was done.

More hours passed. My birth-sore body protested the long hours in the same position in the chair, watching the monitors, watching her pulse-ox fluctuate from seventy-two to eighty-four, but never any higher. Chase eventually left, returning with a couple of pre-made sandwiches, bags of chips, and bottles of soda from the cafeteria.

More coffee, more waiting. Watch her pulse-ox obsessively, willing it to rise. Dozing off fitfully, only to be woken by coughing, by the nurse checking in, by Chase shifting, by my own thoughts.

Mundane things like TV, music, Facebook, Twitter, Instagram...they all fall away when you're in a hospital room, watching your child suffer. All that matters is the bizarre fast-yet-slow passage of time, the monitors, the readouts and the child. The only status that counts is that of your baby.

She breathes, she coughs, she sleeps, she needs a bottle. She shits, and you have to change her without making a mess of the monitor leads. You feed her another bottle, holding her against your chest and feeling guilty for each clean, easy breath you take. You do everything so carefully, so thoroughly, in case that one thing you do just right might just possibly make the difference and get her well sooner. You try to sleep, and can't. Your eyes burn, heavy and hot from exhaustion, but there's no comfort, and even if there was, you wouldn't take it, because to be comfortable while your child lies ill is some kind of betrayal. The hospital room, the whiteboard with its layers of not-quite-erased dry-erase writings, the machines and monitors against the wall, the bevy of wires, the TV on mute, tuned to a local channel and playing soap operas and *People's Court* and *Judge Alex* and now-ancient and partially familiar reruns of *Cheers*. The crib, your baby, finally seeming to be asleep, truly resting, for once not coughing or wheezing and giving you a glimmer of hope, despite the pulse-ox readout of eighty-eight, when you know it has to be at least ninety-five before they'll send her home.

Eventually, a kind of panicked claustrophobia sets in. It's a claustrophobia of time, hour after hour in the tiny room, maybe venturing to the bathroom, choking down food and coffee, listlessly watching crap TV without really caring. You grow desperate for something to change, for healing to occur while you're looking the other way, for the endless monotony to shift. And then you feel guilty for feeling bored when just there she's still gasping, her chest still retracting, because if she's not retracting, she might be getting better.

Eventually Chase made me walk down to the cafeteria, just to get away for a minute. I hated him for making me leave, because I was positive something would happen while I was gone. Interacting with people was an oddity suddenly. I wasn't sure how long we'd been in the hospital. My phone had long since died, and the only marker of time I had was staff shift changes and news broadcasts and which rerun was playing on the TV attached to the wall by a long swivel arm.

In the cafeteria, I ordered two cheeseburgers and watched the cook as he flipped and pressed them. The cook was an enormous black man, easily six foot six and over three hundred pounds, a chef's hat slouched sideways on his head. He moved with a slow, graceful economy, sure and efficient behind the counter. He wore loose clear plastic food service gloves, black and white checkered pants, a white coat-like shirt with two rows of buttons, over which was a spattered apron; his sleeves were spotless, despite the myriad of stains on his apron. He gave me a hesitant smile as he slid the burgers onto buns and put them into styrofoam containers.

"What day is it?" I asked him.

His gaze shifted, and I saw understanding in his eyes. "Thursday. 'Bout seven in the evenin'." His voice was impossibly deep, gravelly, raspy.

"Holy shit," I breathed. "I've been here for two and a half days."

He nodded. "Time turns into somethin' odd in them rooms. Makes you forget just about everythin' but them that's sick." He turned away, pulled the basket of fries out of the deep fryer, and shook them, then dumped them into a pan and sprinkled salt on them before scooping some into the to-go containers and handing them to me. "What'chu here for?"

"My daughter has RSV."

He nodded. "That shit is awful. My youngest had that. Only three months old."

"Mine isn't even two weeks old." I popped a scorching-hot fry into my mouth.

He grimaced. "Goddamn. Sorry to hear it." He scratched his cheek with a huge finger. "She'll be okay, though. They come through it all right. Kids are resilient, you know? They bounce back. She'll be fine. I got four kids, and all but one of 'em got that RSV. They all fine now."

"Thanks," I said. "It's hard to see, sometimes."

"I know it does. It's hard just sittin' there. Can't do nothin'. That's the hardest thing."

I took a deep breath, nodding. "That really is it, isn't it? Being helpless is awful."

"I know that's true." He slapped the top of the counter with his paw and then waved at me. "Your girl'll be fine, and so will you."

I nodded. "Thanks."

I sat down and ate one of the burgers, dipping fries into ketchup squirted out of packets. I was halfway done when someone slid into the chair next to me. It was Anna, in yoga pants and a loose sweater.

"Anna?" I twisted in my seat to give my best friend a hug. "Why are you here?"

She looked like how I felt: faded, exhausted, sore. "Caleb is still in the NICU." She snatched a fry from me. "You?"

"Samantha has RSV."

"Ugh." She snatched another fry, then rubbed one eye with the heel of her palm. "I haven't even seen her, and she's sick."

"Is Niall home, then?" I asked.

She nodded. "Yeah. She's fine. Jeff is home with her. I...I haven't seen him in a week, except in passing. One of us is home, one of us is here."

"This is the first time I've left the room in three days." I'd finished my burger and was picking at the fries, but found I wasn't hungry any longer. I pushed them to Anna, who picked at them as well. "Can you believe this is us? Married, with babies?"

Anna laughed, shaking her head. "No, I really can't. I really can't. I feel like a totally different person than I was three years ago. Even one year ago. You know? Like, was that really you and me going to the bar every night? Getting drunk, hitting on guys?"

I snorted. "*I* hit on guys. *You* always chickened out and made me go up to them alone." I bumped her with my shoulder. "You just sat there watching, sipping your pinot grigio and acting aloof."

"Aloof? Me?" She gave me an incredulous look. "That wasn't me being aloof, that was me being too scared to get off the stool."

"I kinda wish I'd been more scared than I was. That might have saved me from being as much of a skank as I was."

"Yeah, maybe." She said it with straight face, then broke down into snickers of laughter.

I pretended to glare at her. "Very funny, bitch."

"Hey," she said, laughing, raising her hands in a gesture of defense, "I always tell you you're not a skank, and you just argue with me. So this time I agree with you, and you get mad? Pick a feature, hooker."

I laughed with her, and it felt good. "Hey, I'm a girl. I'm allowed." I stood up, and Anna stood up with me. "You should come up and see Samantha."

She nodded. "I'd love to."

Chase was holding Samantha in his arms, feeding her a bottle when we got to the room. As they always did when he saw Anna, Chase's eyes flickered with scabbed-over pain. It didn't bother me anymore—not much, at least. There would always be pain there, I realized. When your husband has a history with your best friend, there would always be an element of buried pain and unavoidable awkwardness. He smiled at us, his face lighting up as his eyes met mine. *That* was what made the awkwardness worth it: His eyes always lit up when he saw me, and a smile always spread on his face when I entered a room.

Anna slathered hand sanitizer on her hands from a dispenser on the wall, then crossed the room to crouch near Chase, touching Samantha's cheek with the back of her index finger. "God, she's adorable. She looks so much like both of you!" Samantha sucked down the last of the bottle, and Chase handed her to Anna, who looked from Samantha to me, and then from Samantha to Chase. "She's got your eyes, Chase, but Jay's nose."

"Thank god for that," Chase said. "She'd have been doomed if she got my nose."

Anna laughed and touched the baby nose in question, speaking in the high-pitched voice people use when talking to babies. "Well, hi there, Samantha. I'm your Auntie Anna. You have to get better so your mommy and daddy can take you home. Just like your cousin Caleb. He's got to get better, too, so you can play together. That's right. You'll have so much fun together, yes, you will."

Chase laughed. "Why do people do that? Talk like that?"

I slapped his shoulder. "Studies have shown that babies register high pitches better—they respond to them better. We do it naturally because we somehow just know it works."

Chase gave me a strange look. "Where'd you learn that?"

"I was stuck with nothing to do but read books and watch TV for *weeks*. I learned all sorts of shit."

Anna handed Samantha back to Chase. "I'd better go. You'd better bring her over as soon as possible, okay?"

"We will," I said. "Now go be with Caleb."

When she was gone, life in the hospital room resumed its pattern. After an unknowable amount of hours, a doctor swept into the room, an older man with delicate hands and wire-framed glasses and steel-gray hair. After a surprisingly thorough examination, he settled Samantha back in the crib and turned to us.

"She's doing very well," he said. "She's on the mend, I'd say. Another day, maybe two, and she should be ready to go home. Her breathing seems clear, her retractions are nearly gone, and she's not producing a lot of mucus. I wish I could let you take her now, but I'd rather keep her for another twenty-four or forty-eight hours, just to be safe. Sometimes they reach this point and then have a relapse. I'd hate to have you go home, only to have to turn around and bring her back."

We both nodded, understanding the logic but not liking it.

"She'll be okay, though?" I asked, my voice embarrassingly tremulous.

The doctor nodded, exuding reassurance. "Oh, yes. She'll be just fine. You'll have to watch her breathing for a while, of course, especially as we get closer to winter. You'll be watching for the retractions along here," he explained, tracing a finger along her diaphragm. "If you see that, this working to breathe, that's when you should bring her in. Hopefully, of course, you won't need to, but that's what you should be on the lookout for, just in case."

He left then, and Chase and I looked at each other in relief. We finally had a goal in sight, an end in view. I settled myself on Chase's lap once again, and he wrapped his arms around me. His breath tickled my ear and my hair; I'd never been so aware of something so simple as breathing. Even relaxed, sitting here on my husband's lap, I was listening to every breath Samantha took, attuned to every sound.

I fell asleep on Chase, and I dreamed a mundane and wonderful dream of rocking Samantha in the darkness of her nursery in our Manhattan brownstone.

Chapter 10: Anna

AFTER TWO AND A HALF WEEKS in the NICU, Dr. Sherman finally let me take Caleb home. Jeff was at our house with Niall, who, he said, was eating and shitting faster than he could keep up with. He sounded slightly hysterical when he said that. I tried not to laugh. I dressed Caleb in a green and white onesie that had a picture of frog on the front, and the words "hop to it.. I buckled him into his car seat, covered him with a blanket despite the eighty-degree July weather, and left William Beaumont Hospital after nearly a month straight. I'd spent most of my time at the hospital, unable to stay away from Caleb for more than a few hours. I knew Jeff was overwhelmed at being alone with a newborn, and I certainly missed him, but I couldn't stomach the thought of something happening to Caleb while I wasn't there.

I clicked Caleb into the seat base, then leaned in to kiss his forehead. His eyes were open, and he tracked me as I closed in on him, batted at me with his little fists. I laughed at him, letting him grip my finger for a moment. I don't think I've ever driven as carefully as that ride from Beaumont to my home. I watched every intersection with paranoia as I passed through, braked early, and accelerated slowly. Normally a twenty-minute ride at the most, it took me over half an hour to get home. When I did, I found Jeff asleep on the couch, Niall on his chest covered in a pink blanket with a burp cloth under her face. Jeff's hands were wrapped around her, his long fingers spanning her body and cradling her in place. A bottle sat on the floor, and the TV was tuned to ESPN.

Caleb was sleeping soundly in his carrier, so I left him there. I gingerly lifted Niall from Jeff's chest and pressed her tiny sweet sleeping face to my breast, breathing in the clean scent of her hair mingling with the faint essence of Jeff. She didn't stir, so I just held her for a few moments, eyes closed, inhaling her presence. My eyes watered, teared up, and I had to quietly sniff them away.

When I opened my eyes, Jeff was awake, watching me with love shining in his eyes. I smiled at him over the top of Niall's head. I set Niall down in her crib in our room, covered her with a blanket, and stood over her, watching to see if she stirred. When I was content that she wasn't going to wake up, I went back into the living room and lay down to slide into Jeff's waiting embrace on the couch. He curled his arms around me and pillowed my head on the crook of his arm. Neither of us spoke for long minutes, content to bask in the glow of being home together.

"I'm finally home," I whispered.

"You're finally home," Jeff murmured in my ear, then nuzzled the hollow of my neck with kisses until I giggled.

His lips trailed kisses around to the base of my throat and upward, planting a blaze of heat deep inside me. My doctor had told me I *should* wait six to eight weeks before resuming sexual activity, but followed that up by saying that as long as I'd stopped bleeding it should be fine, but that he should be gentle. I hadn't told Jeff this, though.

He slid kisses further along my throat to my jaw, then across to my lips, and then we were lost in each other. Of all the kisses I'd ever shared with Jeff, I think that one, lying on our couch with our newborn babies nearby, was the sweetest, most desperate. I'd barely seen Jeff in the previous two and half weeks of Caleb's stay in the NICU, and kisses had been the last thing on our mind in the days leading up to and immediately after giving birth. I kissed him like I'd lost him and then found him again. I kissed him as if I'd been starved of his breath, as if I was drowning and he was my air. I delved into the kiss, lost myself in it. I caressed his face, ran my fingers through his messy hair, rubbed my palms on his jaw, and relished the feel of his stubble under my skin. I breathed a sigh of joyful relief at the wondrous feel of his hands arcing down my spine, at the power of his arms as they cradled me close, at the heady intoxication of his tongue against mine.

He pulled away, leaving us both breathless. "I'm gonna get carried away," he whispered.

"What if that's what I wanted?"

He gave me a puzzled look. "I thought we couldn't for, like, two more months?"

I grinned at him. "I had a C-section. Different rules." I slid against him, insinuating my body into his, pressing my curves into his hardness.

"Oh?" He let his hands wander down my sides to grip my hips and pull me harder against him. "What are the rules, then?"

"As long as I've stopped bleeding, it's fine. You just have to be gentle." I pushed my hands up under his T-shirt to roam his firm stomach and the hard slabs of muscle on his chest. "I stopped bleeding three days ago."

Jeff stared at me, as if assessing my words. "You're sure? I couldn't stand it if I hurt you."

"Just…go slow and gentle, okay?" I angled my body away to push his gym shorts down, freeing his still-swelling erection.

I took his shaft in my hands and caressed him into diamond hardness, and I didn't stop there. I slid my fist around him, toying with him, enjoying the slide of silk around steel, the familiar beauty of his manhood and the way it fit perfectly in my hands. I felt heat welling up inside me, burgeoning into roiling pressure as Jeff's hands found bare skin, pushed away my yoga pants—carefully avoiding my belly and the healing stitches. He delved downward, achingly slow, delicate and tender. The slowness was delicious, building the need inside me to an inferno. He didn't stroke and circle my folds with his customary sureness. No, this time, he explored me with an almost virginal hesitancy, and I delighted in each exploratory touch, each slow swipe.

He knew me too well, though. He still knew how to read my reactions, gauging each gasp and each sigh.

As he worked me gradually into a feverish pitch of need, I did the same to him, caressing his length with my fingers, stroking him with both fists, rubbing his turgid tip with my thumb, tracing the swollen veins and rimming the hollow groove beneath his head with an index finger. Touching him, relearning him, loving him with my hands.

"We have to put one on," I whispered.

He didn't answer; he just reached out to the coffee table a few feet away, slid open the narrow drawer, and withdrew a string of condoms, ripping one free with dextrous fingers. We'd kept some there forever, from when we were merely enjoying each other and not "not trying" to get pregnant. We didn't use them often, but we kept them on hand. Now I was glad we had.

He rolled it on and we shifted on the couch, Jeff's spine against the back of the sofa, me facing him. I spread my leg over both of his and held my breath as he guided himself into me. He stopped when I gasped in surprise at the way he stretched me, holding still until I opened my eyes and resumed breathing. He waited, watching me. I let myself adjust to him, my hands clutching his shoulder and the nape of his neck, my forehead against his. Our eyes locked, and I slowly swiveled my hips to slide him into me, my gaze never wavering from his. It was almost like being a virgin again, tightly stretched, a slightly unpleasant pinch that quickly faded into the familiar ecstasy of his thickness filling me. When he was fully immersed in me, I held tight, not moving, just absorbing his heat and hardness.

Then, with glacial slowness, we began moving, our bodies writhing together in synchronous perfection. He always knew exactly what I needed and was always able to give it to me perfectly. He kissed my neck, my throat, my lips, my shoulder, sliding slowly into me, withdrawing in an achingly tender caress, and then slipping back in again. I could only hold him and gasp, breathe with him, move with him.

When I came, it wasn't an explosion; I slid slowly and inexorably into climax, like an inrushing tide slipping gradually up the beach, wetting the sand further, inch by inch. I clung to Jeff like a shipwreck survivor clutching a spar, holding on to him and gasping breathlessly, ignoring the twinge and ache of stitches pulling, moving my hips with his, hissing as the crest washed over me, whimpering his name as I was left limp and sated. I held tight still as he came with a soft gasp, his entire body shivering with the effort to keep still and slow rather than plunging into me as I knew he wanted to. He stroked deep, gently, stilled there and bit my shoulder, pulled away and gasped my name.

And then Caleb began crying. We both laughed, my head falling forward onto Jeff's shoulder. At first, Caleb just whimpered a bit, a thin mew of just-woke-up displeasure. Then, in the time it took me to disentangle myself from Jeff and re-dress, he had launched into a full-fledged arm-flailing wail of anger.

I unbuckled him from his car seat and lifted him out, cradling him against me, only to realize in a rather messy way why he was crying: He'd blown out his diaper, smearing my hands, arm, and shirt. Jeff laughed, but took Caleb from me and changed him while I cleaned myself off.

In the process, Niall woke up and added to the cacophony with her own quavering infant cries. Having stripped my shirt off and tossed it into the laundry room, I was left in only my bra as I brought Niall out of her crib, discovering with a certain amount of hilarity that she had blown out, too. So I put her on the changing table vacated only moments ago and changed her as Jeff shook a bottle of Enfamil and screwed a nipple onto it.

When Niall was changed and dressed again, I plopped down onto the couch next to Jeff, who watched in fascination as I freed one of my breasts from the confines of the bra and tickled Niall's lips with my nipple. She mewed and nuzzled, worked her mouth, cried in frustration, and then latched on with a vengeance, eliciting a gasp of surprise from me. I felt a tug inside my breast as my milk started.

"That's amazing," Jeff said, watching Niall feed.

"Yeah, it is," I agreed, then glanced at him with a smirk. "You know it means my breasts will be basically off limits for a while, though, right?"

He frowned. "Yeah, that's crossed my mind. I'm not super thrilled with it, but it is what it is."

He paused to set the bottle down and move Caleb to his shoulder, patting his back gently. "As long as I get them back at some point, I'll be fine."

"You'll get them back, don't worry," I said, teasing him. "I might let you play with them sometimes. You'll just have to be careful, 'cause they're super sensitive."

Jeff opened his mouth to reply, but Caleb chose that moment to belch so hard he lurched forward on Jeff's shoulder, sending us both into laughter. Jeff cradled Caleb on his back, supporting his neck with one hand. Caleb's eyes rolled around in his head, searching his surroundings, looking shocked by the massive burp that came out of him.

We passed the day peacefully enough, feeding, changing, burping, and holding the babies, finding a pattern together. It was overwhelming at times, especially when both babies decided to get hungry at the same time, or when they both went apeshit in their diapers together. I also knew the time was coming when Jeff would have to work and I'd be here with them alone, but that was in the future. I held on to the present, clung to the joy of watching the love of my life hold his son, or bounce his daughter in his arms.

I'd thought I was content before, with Jeff. That feeling of being full of love was blown away by the sheer power of my love for my babies. When I finally lay down that first night in my own bed with my husband next to me and my babies in their cribs a few feet away, I felt a peace and happiness wash over me that defied description or quantification. There was simply no holding it in, no way to express it. I was completely flooded by happiness, so overwhelmed by it that I had to turn my face into Jeff's shoulder and cry.

He held me, seeming to understand, or maybe he just knew that sometimes women need to cry and there's just no explaining it. They were tears of joy and happiness, yes, but then, once they were loose and flooding down my face, I found myself also crying from the fear and stress and worry of Caleb's stay in the NICU, being so unsure when he'd get to go home. I'd held it all in while I was there, unable to let it out. Now that Caleb was home, I could cut loose and let myself be weak, let myself feel everything.

Jeff just held me. His arms closed me in, clutched me against him and cradled me, comforted me, soothed me. The storm of tears rocked through me, and Jeff's lips whispered love to me as I wept.

After an unmeasurable time, the flood stopped and I drifted to sleep, nestled in the nook of Jeff's arm, spent from crying, still filled with a happiness I couldn't even begin to describe.

The happiness persisted, even when Caleb woke up two hours later, waking up his sister in the process.

Lying in bed with Caleb suckling at my breast and Jeff feeding Niall a bottle on the other side of me, I thought back to that day so long ago when I'd stumbled out of the Ram's Horn, fleeing uncertain feelings I didn't know how to process for a man I'd just met. My journey had been a convoluted one, that was for sure. I couldn't help wondering where I'd be if I'd decided not to go to the Ram's Horn that day, or if I'd ignored the letter with the plane ticket to New York. Or if I'd stayed in New York and dealt with my fears rather than running from them. Every choice I'd made had led me here, to this moment.

Did I regret anything?

No.

I regretted hurting both Jeff and Chase, in different ways, but that pain had also led us all to this point in time. Chase and Jamie had their own happiness, and I had mine.

Jamie had texted me earlier in evening that the doctor had finally given her the okay to take Samantha home. She'd promised to come over some time in the next week so we could hold each other's babies and catch up some more before she and Chase drove back to New York.

My thoughts fell into a jumble of disordered ideas and slow musings, and then Caleb was done and burped and asleep once more, and I cradled my son to my chest, listening to his breathing, to

Jeff's and to Niall's, feeling my heart swell with an all-encompassing love for my family.

My family.

Once upon a time, I'd given up on ever having a family, on ever having a man love me the way Jeff did.

Which just goes to show you, life is a strange place, a mirror-maze of twists and turns, an incomprehensible adventure in which heartbreak leads to love, in which mistakes lead to perfection, in which tears dry away and reveal the beauty beneath.

Such is my experience, anyway.

The End

About the Author

New York Times and *USA Today* bestselling author Jasinda Wilder is a Michigan native with a penchant for titillating tales about sexy men and strong women. When she's not writing, she's probably shopping, baking, or reading. She loves to travel, and some of her favorite vacations spots are Las Vegas, New York City, and Toledo, Ohio. You can often find Jasinda drinking sweet red wine with frozen berries.

To find out more about Jasinda and her other titles, visit her website: www.JasindaWilder.com.

SNEAK PEEK:

Big Love Abroad

Featuring Ian from *Rock Stars Do It Dirty*

I CLUTCHED THE ARMRESTS OF MY SEAT, staring fixedly out the window to the wet tarmac below. I had my headphones on, Björk playing loud enough to drown out everything else. My breathing was erratic, and I was sweating; we hadn't even finished boarding yet, and I was in the middle of a full-blown panic attack. My black hair was frizzing out from the side of my face and sticking to my forehead, sweat pulling it out of its normally tight ponytail. I hated flying. *Hated*. I'd been on a flight several years back that had gone through such violent turbulence more than half of the passengers had been vomiting by the time we'd made an emergency landing to get out of the storm. I'd never forgotten the helpless horror and nauseating drops in altitude, the way the gusts of wind had tossed us to and fro like a toy.

I didn't have much choice but to take this flight, though. I'd been accepted to the University of Oxford, where I was going to study English literature. I'd recently received my B.A. in lit from the University of Michigan, and now I had a once-in-a-lifetime opportunity to study Jane Austen and the Brontë sisters in the country of their birth. My thesis focused primarily on *Jane Eyre* and *Pride and Prejudice*, and was concerned with how those two works influenced the birth of the romance genre. I had the whole thing mapped out, and had already exchanged emails with a few professors from Oxford over the summer, planning the first steps in solidifying my thesis. I was beyond excited to be moving to England, but first I had to survive the flight.

I felt someone move into the seat next to me. I smelled him first, citrus overtones of some faint cologne, a touch of male sweat, not unpleasantly, and a whiff of copper, like blood, oddly. I turned my head and pulled my Beats by Dre headphones off to hang around my neck.

My heart stopped, and my mouth went dry.

Well, hello, Mr. Chunk o' Hunk...

He wasn't sitting yet, but was facing me as he shoved his carry-on into the overhead compartment. His faded *The Kooks* T-shirt was riding high enough to reveal delectable washboard abs with just a hint of happy trail hair leading down to the Promised Land. I let my gaze slide upward to take in his toned arms flexing as they worked his bag into the compartment, and then his face... oh lordy-lord, he was beautiful. Clean, classically beautiful lines, a strong jaw but not too square or caveman-ish, striking cheekbones and piercing, vivid blue eyes that were somewhere between corn-flower and periwinkle and completely hypnotizing as they flicked down to me.

I was caught staring and flushed red, turning away to stare out the window. We were taxiing now, and he slid into the seat, a pair of iPhone ear-buds trailing down his chest, one stuck into his left ear. He pulled the other bud out and tapped his phone, silencing the faint, tinny music thumping from the dangling earbud. I glanced at him from the corner of my eye, and was mortified to realize he was smirking at me.

Smirking. SMIRKING.

Bastard.

I twisted in my seat to face him, my Latin tem-per flaring at the smug expression on his face. Of course, my temper might have been fueled by my fear and the panic attack I was currently fighting off.

"I don't bite, you know," Mr. Smirky said, with a damnably sexy British accent lacing his words.

"I do."

His smirk widened into a grin. "Well, I might need to get to know you a bit before we start biting each other. You know, exchange names at least." He stuck his hand out. "Ian Stirling."

I shook his hand, noting with an uncomfortable amount of pleasure that his hand was huge and hard and strong, and his nails were well-manicured. Dirty, chewed-up fingernails are a sign of mental laxity to me. An unfair judgment, I suppose, but I just cannot abide a man who cuts his nails to the quick, all squared off and hacked to pieces, or greasy and dirty. I like clean hands. Not dainty, effeminate hands—I like my men as manly as the next girl. Just…manly but *clean*.

As I shook his hand, I noticed the source of the coppery scent I'd noticed when he first arrived: His thumb was bleeding a gash along the cuticle. "You're bleeding," I pointed out, releasing his hand.

He frowned at me, then glanced at his thumb. "Oh, shite. I hadn't noticed. Not sure how that happened." He stuck his thumb in his mouth and sucked the blood off.

I freaked. "That's so gross! Do you know how unsanitary your mouth is? Here, give me your thumb." I grabbed his hand, reaching down into my purse at my feet. I always kept a small first aid kit in my purse. My friends at U of M made fun of me for it, but I liked being prepared for all eventualities.

I'm a type-A person, dominant, prepared, and bossy; or, as my best friend Alexa says, an anal-retentive bitch.

I pulled out my first aid kit, dabbed a dot of Neosporin on the cut, unwrapped a Band-aid, and fixed it to his thumb. "There. All better."

He was smirking again. "Thanks." He said it with a wry tone to his voice, staring at the Band-aid as if he'd never seen one before.

"What?" I asked.

He shook his head. "Nothing."

I crossed my arms under my breasts, which only served to push them up and nearly out of my top. I'm a well-endowed sort of girl, sporting the kind of 36DDD breasts that can only fit in Lane Bryant and Cacique bras. Well, I'm sure there are other stores that sell bras I *could* fit in, but I like nice things, and the way I'm built, there's really only three stores worth shopping at: Torrid, Cacique, and Lane Bryant. The rest of me is fairly well-endowed as well, and for the most part, I own it and I rock it. I'm not afraid to show off what I've got, and I've got a lot to show off. The only time I feel insecure is when guys come around, especially guys like the one sitting next to me. He's the kind of hot who can snag any woman he wants. He could be on the cover of *GQ*. He could stand next to Ryan

Gosling and not feel ugly. Sandy blond hair with hints of red brushed across his forehead, intentionally messy, a bit long in the back, curling in an adorable way. I wanted to tangle my fingers in the slight curls at the back of his neck.

"Not nothing. I heard the tone in your voice." I quirked an eyebrow at him to let him know I was serious. I don't always do the eyebrow lift, but when I do, men obey me. Take that, Dos Equis hot old guy.

He chuckled and waggled his bandaid-wrapped thumb. "I've just not had a Band-aid on since I was boy. It feels a bit odd, is all."

I shrugged. "You were bleeding. There's nothing unmanly about putting on a Band-aid."

"It's a Hello Kitty Band-aid." He delivered the *coup de grâce* deadpan, with an admirably straight face.

I managed to hold my serious expression for a few more minutes. "So?"

"It's pink." Still deadpan, not even a hint of a smile.

"So?"

"So I know real men wear pink, but this might be overdoing it a tad, don't you think?" He finally grinned at me, and we laughed. "And besides, Band-aids in general aren't very manly. Like umbrellas and hand lotion."

"So real men let themselves bleed everywhere, get needlessly wet, and have chapped hands?"

He nodded. "Right."

I laughed. "That's stupid."

He shrugged. "It's what we're taught as men. You're supposed to just deal with whatever happens and be tough." He glanced at the Band-aid again. "But thanks anyway—I do appreciate the gesture, though. You never told me your name, you know."

"Nina Herrera."

He smiled at me, and if I hadn't been sitting down, my panties might have fallen off. "It's a pleasure to meet you, Nina Herrera. So. London?"

I nodded. "I'm attending Oxford in the fall."

"Ah. I had a few mates attended there. Beautiful place." He unplugged the earbuds from the phone and tucked them in the breast pocket of his lavender button-down dress shirt and shrugged out of his dove-gray suit coat. "What are you going to study at jolly old Oxford, then?" He said the last part with an exaggerated Jeeves-the-butler accent.

"Literature. Jane Austen and the Brontë sisters, specifically."

Ian pulled a face. "Ugh. Not my cup of tea, personally. I could never get past the boredom of all the who-said-what rot. Nothing ever really *happened*, you know? Give me Milton or Lord

Rochester any day, if I've got to read boring old English nonsense."

I clutched my chest as if wounded. "Rot? That's the best part! It's all subtle. Every word had so many layers of meaning, everything every person said held importance. The conversations are where everything happens."

He shrugged. "Well, to each his or her own, I guess."

I clutched the armrests again as we began the slow roll down the runway, my chest tightening with pressure as the jet picked up speed. I bit my lip so hard I tasted blood, but it was better than crumbling into hysterics, which was the other option, as the roar of the engines picked up the sense of weightlessness sent my stomach roiling.

"Afraid of flying?" I heard Ian ask.

"Yes. Very," I said, the words clipped out.

"Clearly." He said it with a chuckle. "If you wanted to hold my hand, all you had to do was ask."

I glanced sharply at him. "What?"

He gestured to my right hand, which, instead of the armrest, was gripping his hand. My nails were digging into his flesh, dimpling the skin where each fingernail touched the back of his hand. I forced my hand open and let go, but then Ian reached out and took my hand in his, this time threading our fingers together.

"I'm not fond of flying, either," he said.

I stared at our joined hands, mine small against his, my tan fingers nestled against his fair-skinned ones. He didn't let go, just squeezed my hand gently, and then jutted his chin at my headphones.

"What are you listening to?" he asked.

We were airborne now, but we were still rising steeply and beginning a bank, so my terror ratcheted up even higher as my view out the window angled away from the ground to show nothing but overcast gray sky.

"Björk," I answered, my voice barely audible.

"I love Björk," Ian said. "What's your favorite song?"

"'Pagan Poetry,'" I answered. "But I have to watch the video if I'm going to listen to that song."

"God, that video is brilliant," Ian said, watching me intently, despite his casual conversational tone. "You would look sexy in that dress she's wearing."

I turned to glare at him. "You'd like that, wouldn't you? Seeing me in that dress." I snorted. "I'd be flopping all over the place. It wouldn't be good. I need some serious support for these puppies."

"I would like that, yes." His gaze traveled down to blatantly peruse the "puppies" in question, namely, my breasts.

"Eyes up here, tiger." I pointed at my face, but I said it with a grin, letting him know I wasn't offended by his perusal.

Truth be told, I was all a-twitter inside. He'd *perused* me. Ogled me. He was holding my hand and talking to me, maybe even flirting with me. And he'd checked out my rack. Given, most men did, since it was on display even if I dressed demurely—which I didn't very often—but the way he'd looked me over had almost seemed…like he liked the rest of me, not just my boobs. Usually, a man's gaze took in my breasts, flicked over the rest of me, dismissed me, and then moved on.

Not Ian. He *saw* me; he saw *me*.

And he was still holding my hand, even after the jet leveled out and my nerves receded. This could spell something beautiful, or something heartbreaking, I realized. Maybe both.

Don't miss the rest of
Big Love Abroad
Coming soon!

Made in the USA
Charleston, SC
09 June 2013